Kyleigh's Cowboy

Pamela S Thibodeaux

The Lord appeared to him from afar saying, "I have loved you with an everlasting love; therefore, I have drawn you with loving-kindness." ~ Jeremiah 31:3

Kyleigh's Cowboy
by
Pamela S Thibodeaux

Publisher/Distributor:
Temperance Publishing; an imprint of
Pamela S. Thibodeaux Enterprises, LLC
PO Box 324
Iowa, LA 70647

Cover Design: Get Covers

Published in the Unites States of America
Publishing History: First edition October 18, 2022

Dedication

To my faithful readers and friends. You have guided me along this path for so long and your thoughts, words, prayers, and kindness have played a huge part in **Kyleigh's Cowboy** coming to fruition. I love and appreciate Each and Every ONE of You and pray God blesses you with a rich increase of His almighty good.

Thank You for your continued support!

If you enjoy **Kyleigh's Cowboy** please consider leaving a positive review and posting it at online retailers and websites where readers gather and/or your social media platforms (FaceBook, Good Reads, BookBub, Twitter, etc).

If you haven't already, sign up to receive my **Newsletter** and get a FREE short story.

Chapter One

Kyleigh Winters added a drop of lavender to the dab of coconut oil in her hand and rubbed her palms together. She ran her fingers through her hair and tamed the coarse tresses into a thick braid that reached her waist.

Excitement made her hand tremble, stomach flutter. She took a deep breath to calm the jitters and swiped on mascara, then lip gloss. Something big was bound to happen today. Kyleigh knew and trusted her intuition well enough to recognize the signs which had built into a powerful sense of anticipation over the past few days.

She loved it when God showed up in her life like this. His surprise blessings always manifested at the perfect time.

The morning's prayer list ticked off in her mind. Which one would be answered? A great turnout for their Open House would be wonderful— or maybe a calendar filled with reservations. A long-held, secret desire?

Kyleigh could almost hear the Lord chuckle at her childlike antics. A laugh–deep, carefree, and full of joy— bubbled through her lips.

"I love to hear that." Her daughter, Ramona, walked into the room. "It's been so long since I've heard you laugh that way. I'm glad you're finding a bit of happiness. Are you ready for the Open House?"

Kyleigh hugged her. "Yes. You?"

Her daughter's gaze traveled the room, then settled back on her. "Yes. But if today goes well, we may need to hire additional staff."

The hint of sadness lurking beneath the excitement in her daughter's eyes affirmed to Kyleigh that her child still missed the home she'd grown up in. But the changes they'd made while turning the old ranch homestead into a brand new B&B, complete with horseback rides, hiking trails, hayrides, and campfires had been a desperately needed venture for all of them after Ramona's father died seven years ago.

Kyleigh's joy dimmed with the memory of those first years after her husband passed away. Pain and grief, confusion, and fear smothered them as they struggled to rebuild lives torn apart by tragedy. At first, she'd balked at the idea of turning their vacation home into a place for strangers. But as the bills piled up and income dwindled, the small ranch became a burden...not the haven it was when Dennis bought it years ago with the dream of retiring there. Then Ramona had the idea to sell their homes and invest the money in building a business that hopefully, would sustain the family for years to come. Letting the property go to waste would be a shame, and it would be the perfect place for children when the time came for Ramona and her husband to start a family.

Kyleigh initially reacted with a staunch NO.

Although she'd enjoyed their visits here, she was too much a city girl to consider living in the Texas Hill Country for long periods of time. But the more Ramona talked about the pluses of the move...

A fresh start. A clean slate. A new vision to hold their remaining family together without the harsh memories of her father's sudden and tragic death.

An 18-wheeler had swerved into his lane, cutting Dennis off, sending his car into a tailspin, over the guardrail, and into a ravine. Reminded of the accident every time she passed the spot on her way into the city or returning home, Kyleigh reluctantly agreed to consider her daughter's idea.

And then the insurance check came. Six years after the incident, four years from the court date when the judge awarded the settlement, and two more after numerous appeals and delay tactics. Kyleigh relived the horror of his death when a mail carrier knocked on her door with a certified letter and a check for enough money to catch up on everything she'd fallen behind on and get on with their lives.

But not enough to bring Dennis back.

Never enough for that.

Her daughter's voice pulled Kyleigh out of her reverie. "Us coming here and creating a new life was a great idea, Mom. I know you didn't always see it that way, but Robert and I are glad you finally agreed to give it a try. Maybe now that things are settled, you can think about your future."

Kyleigh shrugged. Mona had urged her for months to get out and socialize more. Though she longed to be a wife again, she had no desire at forty-eight to join the ranks of lonely women trolling bars or online in search of a man. She'd only had one boyfriend before Dennis and the idea of entering the dating pool terrified her. "If

God deems I need another husband, He'll send the perfect someone in His own time."

Ramona laughed and slipped her arm around Kyleigh's waist. "Yeah, but you've got to do your part and get yourself out there."

Kyleigh brushed the familiar arguments away with a wave of her hand. "I'll be happy enough hiring a decent wrangler before we get booked with reservations."

She hooked her arm through Ramona's, and they walked out of the room together as her daughter winked and grinned. "Who knows, he might be a tall, dark, handsome cowboy like dad always fantasized of being."

They laughed. Though Dennis had loved the ranch, he was a city boy to the max, lacking even a sliver of the cowboy gene. And though Robert and Ramona fit in as if they'd been born to the area, Kyleigh had yet to get over the culture shock of moving from New York to Texas.

The women walked from Kyleigh's log cabin to the two-story wood and stone ranch house. Already, guests mingled in the adjoining dining and lodge rooms. More spilled out onto the huge veranda that wrapped around the front and one side of the building.

"Mercy."

Admiration laced Ramona's voice. Kyleigh glanced at her daughter then turned to see what she gawked at. Her son-in-law, flanked by a cowboy, strolled toward them. Her heart did an irrational little twirl, pulse scrambled into high gear. Kyleigh bit back her own murmur of appreciation of the lean physique, muscled forearms and bulging biceps poured into the shirt stretched across a broad chest. Her fingers itched to

8

stroke the salt and pepper hair peeking out from under his hat and curled over his collar. Smooth shaven for the most part, the man's tanned cheeks hinted at a five o'clock shadow just below the surface. *Sexy*. Kyleigh shook herself mentally as the two men approached.

"I think we've found our wrangler," Robert said. "Ladies, meet Lance Stevens. Lance, my wife, Ramona Evans and..." He grinned and bowed low, then rose with a flourish of one arm toward Kyleigh. "Mistress of the Silver Star, my mother-in-law, Kyleigh Winters."

Kyleigh's cheeks heated but used to her son-in-law's teasing, she couldn't stop the hint of smile tugging at her mouth. "I hate it when he does that."

Eyes the color of dark roasted coffee swept over her in a gaze as potent as a caress, then locked with hers. Lance tipped his hat and grinned. A dimple creased his cheek. "Ma'am," he drawled.

Her lips curved in response, and she offered her hand. "Guess it'll take some time to get used to being called that."

Lance eyed her a moment then accepted the handshake. "You're not from here, I gather?"

"No. New York."

"Why, may I ask, did you move all the way from New York to the Texas Hill Country?"

Kyleigh's laugh held a slightly hysterical edge. "I ask myself that daily. So, you'd like to apply for the wrangler position?"

"Yes, ma'am."

"I'm sure you have experience handling horses, but what about people?"

Before he could answer, Ramona brushed a hand down Kyleigh's arm. "We're going to mingle and let you two talk."

Lance tipped his hat and Kyleigh acknowledged her daughter with a nod. "Shall we go into the office?"

He waved her to lead the way.

"You have references?"

He pulled a piece of paper out of his back pocket and handed it to her. Kyleigh murmured a thank you and led him toward the small workplace situated at the back of the lodge next to the restrooms and gift shop. His low wolf whistle tickled her ears.

"Whoa."

Kyleigh turned when his footsteps faltered and saw his gaze riveted to the painting on the wall outside her office door.

"This is amazing. Where'd you get it?"

She tilted her head. "What do you find so amazing about it?"

He stepped closer to the artwork, peered at it a moment then pointed. "At first glance you'd think it was the Star of Bethlehem, but a closer look shows it's merely light reflected off a Texas star. Other than that famous painter of light guy, I've never seen anything like this. So.... brilliant...the way the beams of light play off the rest."

Kyleigh smiled. "That's the best compliment I've ever received. Thank you."

His eyebrows shot up in surprise. "You painted this? You're in the wrong business, honey."

Kyleigh laughed. "I'm not so sure about that. I dabble a bit when I have the time and inclination." She unlocked and opened the door to her office and heard another exclamation of appreciation.

"I haven't seen an office this nice in any place I've worked. Ever. Except maybe my CO's."

A huge L-shaped desk dominated the tiny space. Antique, paned windows let in the afternoon sun and added a warm glow to the rich hue of cherrywood furniture. Short file cabinets—also wood—were tucked beneath wall shelves on one side of the room. On the opposite, keys, room cards and notes graced a large cork board.

Kyleigh indicated for him to take a seat. "Ambience is everything, right?"

Lance situated the chair so that his back wasn't directly to the door. Removing his hat, he waited until she sat before lowering himself into the soft leather cushion. His chuckle sent tremors of awareness through her.

"Yeah. But most people spend their money embellishing the décor of every room *but* the office. This one screams executive, not office manager of a dude ranch."

Kyleigh smiled at the admiration in his tone. "Since I'm both, and I'll be spending the better part of my days in here, I saw no need to scrimp when efficiency and luxury are so easy to combine."

"Not to mention beauty." He ran his hands along the leather inlets of the solid wood arms of the chair.

But his eyes never left her face.

Kyleigh's skin heated at the intensity of his gaze. She blinked to break the hypnotic pull of his enigmatic aura and skimmed the list of references he'd handed her. "I see you've worked all over the country."

"Yes, ma'am, I've been a traveling cowboy for years. Ready to settle a bit though."

"Please, call me Kyleigh. I'm pretty sure we're close to the same age and that makes me not nearly old enough to be a 'ma'am.'"

His chuckle sent her heart into another dizzying tailspin.

"Simply a term used to show manners and respect, but I'll try to remember that, Kyleigh. Pretty name, by the way."

His velvety-rough voice alone could induce erotic fantasies. Kyleigh chided herself for the notion. And for fidgeting. She glanced at the computer to gather her scattered thoughts, then back at him. "We've no reservations as of yet, but if you'd like, we'll schedule a ride or two with Mona and Robert over the next few days and talk salary then."

Lance shrugged. "That's fine. I'm surprised you're opening this late in the year. Fall is a slow time for most guest ranches."

Her sigh spoke volumes. "I know. But I hope having our Open House two weeks before Labor Day will give us a leg-up and a few reservations. I'm planning a big Thanksgiving feast and we'll invite overnight guests as well as day visitors. We'll do the same for Christmas and New Year's. It's all in the marketing, right? And that's where I'm an expert. Or was, before my husband passed away."

He leaned forward, touched her hand. "I'm sorry for your loss, but if it's what brought you here, maybe there's a deeper reason for that too."

Kyleigh stiffened against the waves of pure sensation shivering up her arm. Before she could respond, Ramona appeared in the doorway. "We need you in the kitchen, Mom. We're running out of food. Oh, and bring something to take reservations!"

Kyleigh grabbed a calendar and she and Lance hurried after her daughter.

"What can I do?" Lance asked as they swung through the kitchen doors to find absolute chaos.

"Grab an apron. Start on those dishes while I help Mona prepare more snacks. Robert, take that tray and the calendar out and start booking. Use the note sections if you have to. Be sure and get phone numbers!" she instructed as he strode out the door.

Kyleigh took one more deep breath, said a quick, silent prayer of thanks, then dove into the tasks at hand.

* * * * *

Lance placed a tray of dishes in the washer and rinsed and stacked another to go in next. Between loads, he chopped, fetched, and stirred, taking cues from Kyleigh and Ramona as they whipped up batches of cookies, finger sandwiches, fruit and vegetable trays, and all sorts of hors d'oeuvres. He and Robert kept the drink station filled with tea, water, and lemonade, and the cookie jar replenished as people came and went. The Open House event stretched from mid-morning well into the afternoon and evening.

When the door closed on the final guest, the four of them collapsed around a table and, almost as one propped their feet up on a chair. A bottle of sweet, red wine and four glasses—which he'd grabbed on his way out of the kitchen—sat unopened in the center of the table.

After a moment of the sheer pleasure of being off his feet, Lance opened the wine, poured it, and handed each of them a glass. He raised his in a toast. "If today's any indication, your little B&B with horses—as a local news columnist called the Silver Star—will do just fine."

Glasses clinked. They sipped. Robert raised his in salute to Lance. "To our new wrangler. You went above and beyond the call of duty."

"And not even officially hired," Kyleigh put in.

Lance grinned and sent her a friendly wink. "Wait 'till you get my bill."

The round of laughter muffled into groans.

"So tired it even hurts to laugh," Ramona said as she stood. "And we've got a ton of cleaning to do."

"Leave it," Kyleigh insisted. "We'll get to it in the morning. I think we all deserve a good night's rest. Lance, make yourself at home in whichever room you choose."

She reached into her pocket, then tossed him a master key.

"Tomorrow we'll complete the official," she finger-quoted the word, "'hiring,' then you're welcome to move into the bunkhouse. Unless, of course, you've somewhere else to live."

"Been staying in town until I got hired on someplace. Glad it'll be here."

Everyone said goodnight and went off to their various living quarters. Lance grabbed a duffle bag out of his truck, decided he was too tired to climb the stairs, and chose the nearest exterior room. A hot shower, clean pajama pants, and a comfortable bed eased him into slumber.

A whiplash of lightning followed by the boom of thunder jerked him, shaking and sweating, out of a sound sleep. It took a moment to recognize his new surroundings.

"Just the weather," he muttered, rubbing his chest until his racing heart calmed. "God, help me, it's just the weather."

Chapter Two

Lance awoke to the patter of rain against the windowpane. Softer now. Gentle. Nothing of the raging elements that woke him earlier. He took a moment to relish the quiet and stretch his aching muscles. He glanced at his watch. 6:30. Later than he'd slept in months. A rarity. Other sounds penetrated the silence. The echo of hooves on rock. The creak and swoosh of a door followed by the clatter of dishes. The hum and whine of the dishwasher. His room, located on the backside of the kitchen, made it easy to hear the activity therein. He tumbled out of bed and pulled on clean clothes. The moment he stepped out into the moist, morning air, Robert whistled from the corral and waved him over.

He greeted the other man with a handshake. "Morning. Up and at 'em early, I see."

Robert chuckled. "Mona's always up early, which means I am too. Kyleigh will sleep in a while. I hope."

Lance's gaze followed Robert's when the other man looked toward his mother-in-law's cabin, a hint of concern creasing his brow. "Anything I should know there?"

Robert handed him a bucket and gestured for him to climb up on the ATV seat. He maneuvered the vehicle through the corral, scooping feed from the sack into individual containers for the horses tied in their spots.

"Dennis's death—that's Ramona's dad—has been hard on her. She fumbled around, lost, and aimless. for years."

"She seemed pretty together yesterday, considering all the chaos."

Robert grinned. "Once upon a time she thrived on chaos, although this will certainly be a different kind. It's not the commotion, but the lack of it we're concerned about. Dennis was born in the city and flourished there, but he loved coming here for vacation and holidays. He enjoyed the wide-open space, the vastness, the peace and quiet, and really looked forward to retiring here. Kyleigh, on the other hand, merely tolerated it, often hoped he'd change his mind. She loved the hustle and bustle of city life and the challenges of being a top-notch marketing executive. It took us a lot of talking to get her down here like this. We just worry."

"Well, we'll just have to make sure she stays busy when possible and learns how to relax the rest of the time."

Robert chuckled. "Good luck with that. So, tell me more about yourself."

Lance shrugged. "Not much to tell. Married once, grown son. Relationship went south during my second stint in Afghanistan. Haven't seen the ex in years. Very little contact with the boy, either. Honorable discharge from the service about ten years ago, been a roaming cowboy ever since."

"A man of few words. Not sure how that'll work with guests."

Robert's grin took the sting out of his comment, but Lance knew from experience a lack of emotion in describing his life made people even more curious. But truth takes trust. "Don't worry, I can be chatty when I need to."

Robert's short bark of laughter rang out in the morning air. "What makes you think your roaming is over?"

"Been thinking of settling down for quite some time now. Looking for that place that calls to the soul if you know what I mean. Felt it the moment I drove through the gate."

"Really?" Robert asked. Curiosity arched his brow.

Again, Lance shrugged. "Hard to explain something not everyone understands."

"I agree. Dennis always said that about this place. Ramona and I have too."

"But not Kyleigh?"

Robert shook his head. "I think she's settling in a little more now that the renovations are over and we're actually opening. Who knows though, right?"

Conversation trailed off as they finished feeding the horses. Robert showed Lance how things were set up in the tack room, where the cleaning supplies were and how to log medications, as well as veterinarian and farrier visits.

"Got someplace I can keep my horse separate until he gets used to the herd and they, him?"

Robert pointed to a small corral next to the bunkhouse. "You might need to check the fences and gate, but that should work."

"Great. Thanks."

A cowbell sounded. Robert grinned, then slapped Lance on the shoulder in a friendly gesture. "Breakfast."

The two men went into the lodge where Ramona had laid out a virtual feast—eggs, biscuits and gravy, hash browns, mini-pancakes, sausage patties.

"Whoa, you trying to feed an army?" Robert asked with a laugh.

She grinned. "Getting used to cooking larger amounts. Mom, breakfast is ready!"

"She's up?" Lance asked.

"Yes, she's up," the woman in question remarked from the door. "Someone's got to call all of those people who signed up for reservations and get them scheduled. A few want to come as early as next weekend. You guys think we're ready?"

"Ready as we'll ever be," Robert assured. "We'll just book small numbers until we hire the additional staff if we have to, but we're ready."

"Sounds like a plan." Kyleigh gathered her dish and utensils, then began preparing her plate.

Lance watched her from the corner of his eye and fought back a grin at the meager amount of food she put on the tray. *Barely enough to feed a bird.* Helping himself to generous portions, he waited until Kyleigh sat, then joined her at the table. Robert and Ramona soon followed. He removed his hat and bowed his head while they said grace, then dug in. A hum of pure satisfaction escaped before he finished the first bite. "Where did you learn to cook?"

Ramona smiled. "Culinary school. I've dreamed of owning a B&B or restaurant since I was a little girl."

"This is amazing. There's something different in the eggs and pancakes. What's your secret?"

She laughed. "Can't tell, it's classified."

Lance chuckled. "I've kept classified information secret before, but I respect your privacy."

"You were in the military?"

He nodded. "Marines."

"Oh, wow. Well, thank you for your service."

He acknowledged her comment with an inclination of his chin and continued eating, praying he hadn't said too much. He hated to be questioned as to his duties, where he'd been, etcetera. Once they'd finished the meal, he followed Kyleigh into the office to complete his paperwork for hire.

She handed him a clipboard with the essential documents attached and an employee handbook. "I know Robert wants you to go with him on a trail ride, so if you want to just fill out the official application and sign the necessary waivers, you can read the handbook and I'll answer any questions you might have later."

"You want me to take this into the other room?"

She smiled and his heart stumbled. "Wherever you're more comfortable."

He pulled the chair closer to her desk and made quick work of the forms. "These seem pretty standard. Is there anything special I should know?"

"My biggest concern is that everyone, and I mean *everyone* know and understand the rules for putting a guest on a horse. The age, height and weight regulations are non-negotiable."

"What about this one on kids under six? Some learn to ride younger than that. Hell, some are rodeoing younger than that."

She arched a brow at him. "Our liability insurance does not allow children under six years of age to go on a trail ride. Period."

The fire in her eyes set one ablaze in his blood. Lance resisted the urge to reach over and smooth the frown from her face. He smiled, tipped his hat. "Yes, ma'am."

Her lips curled in response. "I know some ranches make exceptions and maybe once we've been in operation for a while, I will too. But for now, we need to stay on the up and up. We're too new and have put too much money into this endeavor to get into trouble this early in the game."

Lance wanted nothing more than to linger and share pleasantries with her, but Robert waited at the barn. He stood, shoved the handbook into his back pocket. "Well, guess I need to get on out there and ride along with Robert."

"Have fun."

He nodded, turned on his heel. "Yes, ma'am."

"Oh, and Lance?" She waited until he swung back to face her before continuing. "I thought we'd agreed last night to cut the 'ma'am,' and just call me Kyleigh."

"Yes, ma'am." He chuckled, winked, and left to meet Robert at the corral, leaving his lovely boss and Ramona to complete their domestic duties.

His laugh reverberated in her mind and Kyleigh found herself smiling at odd times during the remainder of her morning. She'd just finished entering Lance's information into her payroll/accounting program when Mona radioed and announced it was time for a coffee break. Keying the mike, she replied, "Sounds lovely. I'll meet you in the dining room." She got there as Mona set their cups on the table alongside two slices of sponge cake topped with cinnamon streusel. "Mmmm, early dessert always works for me."

Ramona laughed. "The cake is left over from the parfait I made for lunch. I whipped up the streusel topping just for us."

Kyleigh bit into the crunchy sweetness and hummed with pleasure. The two chatted amiably over the treat, then Mona scooted back from the table and picked up their cups. "So, what do you think of Lance?" she asked walking to the drink station. With both of them filled and steaming, she sat, nudged her chair closer and leaned in with a conspiratorial whisper. "Kinda sexy if you ask me."

Kyleigh laughed. "Which I didn't, out of respect for your *husband*."

Ramona giggled. "I may be married but I'm not dead." She hissed in a breath when Kyleigh winced. "Sorry, Mom, that cliché can be insensitive. You know what I mean though."

"It's ok, sweetheart. The fact your father is no longer with us still stabs me in the heart unexpectedly. But yeah, maybe we could change the cliché to 'blind' or—on second thought, just not use it at all. It tends to be insensitive no matter what word is substituted."

"True. I believe Dad would be proud of what we're doing here."

"I'm sure he is," Kyleigh agreed. She surveyed the room. Concentration furrowed her brow. "I also think we need to hire at least one more person to help with housekeeping and cooking. You can't do it all and I'll be busy in the office."

"No worries. We've got a stack of applications. You call in those you'd like to consider, and I'll meet with them after you. Meanwhile, I'm going to get that kitchen cleaned and mop the floors."

"Deal."

"But you still didn't answer my question."

Kyleigh returned her gaze back to her daughter. "Which is...?"

"What do you think of Lance?"

Kyleigh thought about his dark, expressive eyes, strong jaw, and chiseled features. His sense of humor. Not overly tall, he topped her five foot, three inches only by about six, but he filled out his western shirt and jeans in a way that did things to her libido she hadn't felt in years. Though she wouldn't tell her *daughter* that. She pushed back from the table, stood. "I'll say he is handsome and seems quite nice. Any more will have to wait until I get to know him better."

Ramona rolled her eyes and muttered, "Hopeless."

Kyleigh grinned and patted her daughter's cheek then headed into the office leaving Mona to finish her coffee and stew or get started on her cleaning.

At noon, the four of them gathered around the lunch table and enjoyed another of Ramona's delicious meals.

Beef tips, potatoes with gravy—both white and brown— homemade rolls, and vegetable medley filled the lodge with mouthwatering aromas and the chocolate parfait graced the snack table.

"Man, we eat like this every day, none of us will get on a horse."

Lance laughed at Robert's prediction. "Trust me, buddy, once you get busy, you'll want meals like this. I've worked enough ranches in the past ten years or so to know that for sure."

"Where all have you been?"

Lance finished the last bite of his food and leaned back in the chair. "I've traveled all across the states and overseas. Worked in the pipeline industry from the time I was seventeen till twenty-two and then joined the Marines. Stayed in for the next twenty years, retired and worked as a wrangler or ranch hand since from Montana to Oklahoma, Wyoming to Texas and a few places in between."

"Wow, must be wonderful to see so much of the world. Mona and I had planned to travel."

Robert visibly winced at his faux pas when Kyleigh declared, "We'd have never started this venture had I known you two wanted to travel."

"I mean, we plan to travel in the future after the kids are all grown and gone."

Lance's chuckle dispelled the sudden tension clouding the air. "When's the baby due?"

Color bloomed in Ramona's cheeks. "Oh, we've got plenty of time for that."

"I don't know...never put off until tomorrow...." The shrill of the telephone cut off the remainder of his words.

Ramona jumped up. "I'll get it."

Lance turned to Robert as she rushed off to answer the call. "How old are you two, anyway?"

Robert laughed. "Please don't say Mona could pass for twelve. She doesn't mind looking younger than her twenty-four years but showing her driver's license gets old. I'm twenty-five."

"How long y'all been together?"

"Since junior high."

"Wow, long time."

Robert grinned at him, then winked at Kyleigh. "Yep, lots of folks thought we wouldn't make it past high school, especially with me an orphan raised in a home for troubled boys. But look at us now. An old married couple, part owners in a business, Mona in her element as a chef. Just can't get any better than this—except having a kid or two, which we're hoping to do in the next few years. Who knows? We might even have twins and get our boy and girl in one fell swoop."

"Wouldn't that be wonderful?" Kyleigh pushed back from the table and cleared away the plates then set out their dessert bowls.

Lance's brow quirked at the hint of reprimand in the otherwise sweet tone. He could tell Robert heard it too when the younger man lowered his gaze and sipped his drink, a flush staining his cheeks. *Wonder what the story is there?*

Before conversation resumed, Ramona returned from the office with two more reservations booked.

After indulging in the best chocolate parfait he'd ever tasted, Lance helped clean the corral and tack room while the ladies washed the dishes, then moved his belongings into the bunkhouse. He spent the rest of the afternoon tightening barbed wire along the fenced enclosure and hinges on the gate. Satisfied the small pasture would hold his horse, he drove to town, picked up Champ and brought him back out to the place they'd call home for the time being.

* * * * *

Labor Day weekend turned out to be as fun as it was educational. Though not booked solid, there were enough guests to keep everyone on their toes and busy from dawn till 'dark thirty,' as Robert deemed the late hours. Kyleigh and Ramona were still in the market for someone to help in the kitchen and with housekeeping, which meant Lance and Robert filled in whenever and wherever necessary in the days to follow.

Today though, Lance was ready for a nice, long ride. Alone. Away from people. Having only a couple of guests at the time allowed him the freedom to take a day off and do so.

He stepped out of the bunkhouse and glanced toward Kyleigh's cabin where she sat on the porch. An easel blocked his view of her pretty face. *Maybe I won't ride alone after all.* He headed in her direction.

"Morning." He hesitated on entering her creative sphere without permission, horror stories of interrupting an artist at work running through his mind. She glanced up, smiled, and his pulse scrambled.

"Morning. How are you today?"

"Great. Just getting ready to head out for a ride. Want to tag along?"

Kyleigh grinned and shrugged with a slight shake of her head. "I'm not much of a rider."

"What? You own a guest ranch, and you don't ride? We're going to have to fix that," he declared with a chuckle.

"Maybe, but not today."

"What'cha working on? Or am I allowed to ask?"

She laughed. "I'm not one of those crazy, eccentric artists who doesn't want her work looked at until it's perfected. C'mon up and tell me what you think."

Lance ascended the steps then stopped, awestruck by the images on her canvas. Wildlife grazed on lush green tufts of grass peeking through rocks and dirt. Brightly colored birds flitted from tree to tree. Bees and butterflies feasted on the nectar of Prickly Pear Cactus and Purple Passion flowers. A waterfall fed the rapids rushing over slabs of stone then settled in a soft pool of aqua as smooth as glass. "It's Pedernales Falls."

The surprised pleasure on her face sent a horde of butterflies bouncing off his ribcage. "You've been there?"

He nodded. "Yeah, I try to visit area state parks as often as I can. Camped there a time or two in between jobs."

"You've lived in the Hill Country for a while now, haven't you?"

"A few years."

"And you love it?"

Lance nodded again. "I've seen majestic mountains, rolling hills and desert sands but there's just something intimate and cozy about the Hill Country."

"You sound like Dennis," Kyleigh remarked with a sigh. "He loved this area. Looked for years to buy a place and when this one came open, snatched it up."

"Sounds like your husband was a great guy. Wish I could've met him."

Pleasure lit her ebony eyes so the lighter colors within the irises shone through. "You would have loved him—everyone did. And I'm sure you two would have made great friends."

Their gazes locked. The air pulsated between them. Desire, sharp and painful stabbed in his blood. *Easy boy,* he chided himself then tipped his hat. "I'll take that as a compliment. Guess I'd better head out if I'm going to take that ride. Sure you don't want to come along?"

"Not this time, but thanks."

"We'll take a rain check then." He turned his horse and left before he did something stupid. Like drag her into his arms and kiss her senseless.

Two days later, glad to see no easel or painting in sight, he rode up with another horse saddled and in tow as Kyleigh settled into the rocking chair on her porch. "I'm calling in your rain check."

"I told you I'm not much of a rider. I'm not comfortable enough on a horse to tackle these hills."

Lance dismounted and looped Champ's reins over the porch rail and held a hand out to her. "We'll stay on flat land then."

She blew out a breath. "You're not going to take no for an answer, are you?"

He grinned. "No, ma'am."

Kyleigh pushed herself out of the chair with a sigh. "Let me get my boots on and grab a hat."

Five minutes later he helped her mount and adjusted her stirrups, lingering a moment when his hand grasped her calf to check the length. "Good?"

She nodded and he handed her the reins. Awareness sizzled from the simple brush of hands in the exchange. Sensing her hesitation and fear, he swung into his saddle, turned Champ alongside her horse and put his hand over hers. "Trust me."

A smile broke through her tense lips, her shoulders relaxed. "I do."

Ramona and Robert stared out the lodge window in total shock. "He's got her on a horse," Mona whispered.

Robert laughed. "Yeah. That's a good sign. Right?"

She beamed at him. "The best."

Chapter Three

Lance saddled Champ and headed out of the corral on his first trail ride as lead wrangler. Robert rode drag. They'd been over the trails daily for more than a month now, and he'd yet to go solo. He understood protocol and chain of command and resisted the urge to buck the system—a lesson he'd learned well during his stint in the military. Ramona and Kyleigh had hired a sweet young woman to help with housekeeping, cooking, and serving. Elaina Maynor fit right in with the rest of them but did little to hide her interest in him. As a result, Lance stayed on edge more than he cared for. Or cared to admit.

Not that she wasn't a lovely creature...lustrous honey-gold tresses, blue eyes that sparkled with life and mischief, lips that would tempt a saint—which he wasn't but heck, at twenty-something she was young enough to be his daughter— and long, thin, brown legs toned from years of running and yoga. This he knew because he'd seen her out more than once on the hiking trails and down by the pool. Today she'd tagged along on the trail ride and kept the guests engaged with laughter and flirtation.

Teenage boys nearly toppled over themselves to garner her attention, yet her eyes bore a hole in his back.

"Y'all ready to pick up the pace a little?" he called over his shoulder. A chorus of agreement rent the still, morning air. "Ok, here we go!"

Lance kicked his horse into a trot, then a slow lope, rounding bends and slipping through the trees. Once they reached a plateau, he urged his mount into a light gallop, then gradually slowed back to a walk when they started on an uphill climb. He stopped and turned as the others caught up. He stroked a hand down the blonde mane of his sorrel gelding and whispered to soothe the horse's impatient nature. "We still got everyone? James? Jack? Crystal? Bob?"

"Not worried about losing me?" Elaina shouted, a hint of teasing in her tone.

"I'm bettin' you can hold your own. Robert too," Lance added, careful not to single her out or show too much enthusiasm.

When the allotted time for the ride neared its end, he shuffled the riders back into the corral and obliged them with pictures and conversation. He laughed when the boys handed him a tip while kissing their horse as the sign posted on a tree encouraged: *If you enjoyed your ride, kiss your horse, and tip your guide. Or vice versa.*

Elaina leaned in for the vice versa but he sidestepped her advance.

"Staff doesn't tip staff."

Her mouth turned down in a pretty pout, but he ignored that too, hoping she'd get the message soon enough that he was not interested.

In her, anyway.

Kyleigh, on the other hand, never strayed far from his thoughts.

Besides, he had no desire to start another family, and hooking up with a woman half his age was bound to do just that.

She flounced off, muttering under her breath.

"She's got it bad." Robert's voice broke through Lance's thoughts.

"Yeah, and doesn't take hints very well, or even a downright 'no' for that matter."

"Want me to talk to Mona or Kyleigh?"

Lance shook his head. "I can handle my own. But thanks."

"Ok, but if things get too sticky or uncomfortable, let me know. Can't risk any trumped-up charges of sexual harassment or anything."

Lance chuckled. "I won't file any."

Robert had the grace to grin and punched him on the shoulder. "You know what I mean...woman scorned and all that...."

"I get your drift and I'll keep my guard up."

This set the tone for the next several weeks. Although they weren't overwhelmed, guests came and went in a steady stream. Kyleigh's marketing genius paid off when their idea of a haunted house, complete with ghost stories around the campfire and costume contests, sold out the entire week leading up to Halloween and for several days after.

When the last guest vacated their cabin, the staff collapsed around the lodge room for a much-needed and well-deserved break.

Ramona stretched and groaned. "I hurt in places I never knew existed."

Robert tugged her close to his side on the couch they occupied. "You and me both." He kept a hand on her hip, but raised his gaze to Lance. "What'cha gonna do on your days off?"

Lance shrugged. "Haven't thought that far out. Might go to Boerne or Bandera for a couple of days." Before he could say more, Kyleigh strode from the office and handed him the phone and a piece of paper.

"Urgent message. Feel free to use the office for privacy."

He thanked her and walked into the tiny room, closing the door behind him. What the call revealed left him nauseous and sweating. He fumbled with the door, stumbled through, and all but slung the phone at Kyleigh. "Sorry to leave you in a lurch, but I gotta head out."

"What's up?" Robert asked.

Lance swallowed the hard knot of bile in his throat. "My old platoon took a direct hit. I gotta go."

Sorrow filled Robert's eyes. "Oh, man, no worries. We're not too slammed until Thanksgiving week. You don't worry none, your job will be waiting when you get back."

Kyleigh's soft touch on his arm sent a measure of calm through Lance's veins. "What can we do?"

"Pray this damn war ends soon. I'll call." With that, he hurried to the bunkhouse and threw together a duffle bag of enough clothing for a few days.

Kyleigh waved him down on his way out. Sympathy lit her gaze. "Here's your check. Holler if we can do anything for you."

Lance caressed her cheek with his fingertips. "Thanks. I'll be back. Ask Robert to see about Champ."

She nodded.

Lance eased his truck into drive and left her standing in the parking lot, brushing away the dust from his wake.

* * * * *

Less than an hour later, Lance boarded a plane for D.C. This wasn't the first funeral he'd attended over the years since he'd retired from the Marines. As long as his friends remained enlisted, he had the sinking feeling it wouldn't be the last. A familiar sense of angst rose in his chest. *Why won't they just retire and let the young men come in to fight this stupid war? How much longer will our government sacrifice its sons and daughters for a hopeless cause? Why does God allow such atrocities?*

The three-hour flight passed without incident. Lance disembarked, gathered his duffle bag, and hailed a cab to the funeral home where the service was set to start at 8:00 a.m. the next morning. Family members gathered around a flag-draped casket. Tears and sorrow laced the atmosphere with desolation and the heavy scent of despair. He took a breath and walked to his comrade's widow. Words were never his strong point, so Lance held her while she sobbed into his chest. Later they sat in the cafeteria where she regaled him with memories of his friend's last leave, their final conversation. The unkept promises.

"Why didn't he retire when you did? I kept begging him to, but he felt he could be of service to the younger men and women."

"I don't know, Ellen. I've tried talking each member in my band of brothers and sisters into retiring. Some veterans are one-time enlistees, some serve their twenty or twenty-five and get out and others are lifers. I don't get it either. No one really knows the reason lifers are committed until death. It's just in their blood, I guess."

"Well, now his blood is spilled on the same cursed soil as so many others, and I'm alone! What am I going to do?"

"Wish I had all the answers you need right now. I don't. Doubt anyone does. But they will come in time."

He told her about the ranch and extended an invitation, making a mental note to let Kyleigh know he'd done so.

As usual, when he left one of these events, Lance felt he'd done all he could do to honor his brother or sister-in-arms and yet, never enough. The helpless anger didn't dim with time, only embedded deeper into his soul until he wondered if he would ever be whole again.

Kyleigh's face glided across his mind and his heart took flight. *Maybe there is hope.*

If both of them could let go of their pasts long enough to embrace a future.

Within three days of leaving the Silver Star, he was home and back on a horse fending off Elaina and wishing for something he might never have....

Freedom. And a love so rare and precious, nothing short of eternity could sever it.

* * * * *

Kyleigh walked along the hiking trail in the waning twilight as the ranch settled in for the evening. Laughter and song flowed on the breeze from the few guests gathered around the campfire. The pleasure that tingled through her at the sound of Lance's hearty chuckle was quickly choked off by a swift tug of agitation at Elaina's high-pitched giggle. *The woman acts like a silly teenager when she's around him.*

Kyleigh took a deep breath and quelled the nasty thoughts.

Dennis's voice rose in her mind. *Why does she bother you so much?*

"I don't know," Kyleigh muttered and settled herself on a huge rock. A warm light enveloped the area next to her.

Yes, you do, and it's OK to have feelings for him, Kyleigh. It's been more than seven years now. Time to let me go and find the happiness you deserve.

"I was happy with you."

We were happy together, sweetheart, and I had no desire to leave you so soon. But that is something we have no control over.

Her breath hitched in a sharp, painful wail. "I still don't understand!"

We're not meant to understand, but trust. Trust that God has a plan and a purpose for your life.

"You were my plan and our home, family, and my job were my purpose."

No, Kyleigh. I was your husband. Robert and Ramona will grace you with more family. This ranch is your purpose now. Use your degree and that incredible talent you have to make it shine. Shine my darling. Shine....

She began to weep as the light of his presence faded into absolute darkness. "Dennis? Dennis!"

Lance glanced up; his ears tuned to what sounded like someone crying. There it was again. *Dennis!* His heart tripped into hammer-like beats. "Where's Kyleigh?"

Robert paled in the firelight. "I thought she was home."

Again, the cry reverberated on the still night air. Lance scrambled from his seat and grabbed the flashlight they kept stashed by the pit for times when they had trouble starting or keeping the fire going. "Get Mona in case she's hurt."

He took off at a run. "Kyleigh!" Something or someone stumbled and slipped. Sobs rent the air. Rocks slid down the hillside. "Kyleigh, stop!"

"What?"

"Just stop! Let me come to you. Where are you? Which trail did you take?"

"I'm on the path behind the lodge."

"Are you hurt?"

"No." But her voice quivered.

"Kyleigh...."

"I'm OK, just a little shook up. It got so dark, so fast."

"Hang on, I'm on my way. Keep talking." Lance continued to climb toward her voice, cursing the moonless sky. *God, help me find her and keep her safe. Please. I know we haven't always been on the best of terms but I'm begging You...."*

Relief weakened his knees when his light bounced off her boots. He shone the beam up her legs and into her tear-drenched face. His heart twisted at the fear and anguish in her lovely, ebony eyes. "I'm here," he whispered and hurried to gather her against his side while she soaked his shirt with tears.

"I.... I'm sorry...."

"What are you doing out here alone—and so late in the evening?"

"I hadn't planned on going far or staying long, then Dennis...." Her words trailed off. She shivered and struggled with her emotions. "I got turned around and lost my way."

He brushed back her hair in a soothing gesture. "It's OK. I've got you. You're safe now."

Robert and Ramona's voice rang out. "Mom!"

"Kyleigh!"

Lance whistled. "I'm with her. We'll be down in a minute! Are you ready? Can you walk?"

She nodded and moved to stand but her ankle gave way.

Lance handed her the flashlight, then scooped her up in his arms and together they made it back down the hill without falling. Ramona held the door while he settled Kyleigh on a chair in the lodge-room, then removed her boot. "Ankle's a little swollen. We need some ice. Anti-inflammatory cream...over-the-counter meds if you have them. A bandage and pillow."

She and Robert rushed to do his bidding. He propped Kyleigh's foot up on a stool and held the ice pack on it for twenty minutes, then wrapped it after applying the cream.

Ramona handed her mother a glass of water and two pills, then turned to her husband. "Looks like we'll need to grab those crutches we found in the attic."

"Oh, no, I'll be fine."

Lance dared a grin at the defiant lift to her chin. "Sure, you will. We'll make certain of it. You lead the way and I'll carry her home," he told Ramona, then swept Kyleigh up once more while Robert went back out to sit with the guests until time to shut things down for the night.

Chapter Four

Lance strode into the lodge via the laundry room and punched his timecard into the clock. Thanksgiving week loomed ahead with no rest in sight. They were booked solid from the weekend before through the weekend after.

The door opened behind him and the hair on the back of his neck stood on end. He turned and barely managed to sidestep Elaina as she sidled up close to him.

"Mornin', Cowboy," she crooned.

He tipped his hat. "Morning."

She blocked his exit, so Lance spun on his heel and headed out through the kitchen with her close behind.

"Why do you keep avoiding me?"

"Just busy."

"Bull. You're either running away or ignoring me. I know you think I'm pretty, Lance, and that you're attracted to me." She clamped a hand on his shoulder to halt his steps.

He twisted and held out an arm to keep her from colliding with him. "Doesn't matter whether I think you're pretty, I'm not open to your suggestions, Elaina."

"I don't know why you keep avoiding the issue. We're going to end up together. Just hide and watch."

He nudged her back a notch. "Not on your life, little girl."

Her low growl followed him out the door.

"Everything all right?" Kyleigh chose that moment to walk into the dining room. She'd hesitated to enter before now, not wanting to interrupt. She hadn't wanted to eavesdrop either, but could not tear herself away from their conversation or the tension in the air.

Elaina huffed. "He treats me like a child."

Sympathy pushed through the frustration she had toward the other woman. "Well, there are lots of years between you two."

"Age is just a number."

"True, but some people don't feel that way, Elaina. He's old enough to be your father. I know some men bask in having a younger woman on their arm. Others don't. We have to respect that."

Instead of the acquiescence, she'd hoped for, Elaina turned on her in an angry whirl. "You're just jealous cause you want him for yourself! I've seen the way he looks at you and you at him when you think no one notices. And all that getting lost and hurting your ankle...."

"That's enough young lady! You can button it up or pick up your check and get off my ranch," Kyleigh snapped, then whirled around and stormed into the kitchen. The door slammed in her wake.

"What's going on?" Ramona asked.

"Elaina better get an attitude adjustment really quick or we're going to be in a bind. You hire a couple of extra hands for Thanksgiving Day?"

"Yes."

"Get them on standby in case she quits."

"You want to tell me what happened?"

Kyleigh rolled her eyes and bit back the angry retort stinging her tongue. "Let's just say a major difference of opinion that involves another staff member."

Ramona dared a laugh. "She's hot after Lance and you don't like it."

"I don't like the way she throws herself at him with no respect for his feelings or opinion on the age difference between them. If he'd shown her the slightest encouragement, I wouldn't give a damn, but he hasn't. He's done everything within his power to politely decline her advances and when I tried to reason with her, she got all snarly. I will not have insubordinate employees on this ranch. Nor will I tolerate a woman who can't handle her lust outside of work. I know she's not much older than you, but she acts half your age, and I won't put up with it another minute."

They turned when Elaina opened the door. "I'm sorry, Ms. Kyleigh. I was out of line. I don't want to quit, and I don't want you to fire me. I really need this job. It's just...I love him."

"You can't possibly love him, Elaina." Kyleigh sighed. "You barely know him."

"But I do. I can't explain it and that's the problem! He won't even give me the chance to *get* to know him. He just keeps shooting me down."

"Well, maybe you should take the hint that he's not interested and look elsewhere."

Elaina had the grace to look sheepish. "Yes, ma'am. What's next for me to do?"

Kyleigh accepted her apology with a curt nod. "If you've finished what we had on the schedule for today, you're free to go. Take the afternoon off and get a massage or something. Clear your head. We'll see you in the morning."

"Yes, ma'am."

"Elaina?" When the girl faced her once more, Kyleigh softened her tone. "Unrequited love is not worth throwing away your dignity and self-respect."

Color bloomed in the younger woman's cheeks. Elaina acknowledged Kyleigh's comment with a slight tuck of her chin and turned to go. A collective sigh echoed when she walked into the laundry room, clocked out, and left.

* * * * *

Lance looked up as Kyleigh scooted back from the staff dinner table and addressed him. "Lance, can I see you in the office once you've finished eating, please?"

"Sure. I can come now."

"No need. Eat. Get some dessert. I'll see you in a few minutes." With that, she left the room.

Well... hell... Feel like a kid summoned to the principal's office. "Either of you guys know what I've done to have the boss call me into her domain?"

When Ramona and Robert shook their heads, he rose from his seat, put his dishes in the bin, and grabbed two plated servings of chocolate cake from the dessert table.

Robert laughed. "Going in prepared to soften her up, I see."

"Yeah, but I've no idea why or what for." He carried the cake with him, paused for a moment and watched her through the paned glass inserts in the top half of the door.

She stood before the corkboard, eyes scanning, then reached up to unpin a note. Lance's heart stumbled when the material of her jeans and T-shirt tightened across her soft frame from the movements. He swallowed hard and tapped the closed door with his toe. Kyleigh bid him entrance then, seeing his hands were full, opened it.

"You didn't have to bring me dessert, but thank you."

"What's up?"

She sat down, waved for him to take a seat then lifted her fork and bit into the decadent creation her daughter had whipped up. She arched a brow when Lance moved his chair from across the desk to beside it, but forked up another morsel before saying anything else. "I overheard your conversation with Elaina this morning."

"Wonderful," he muttered, then shoved a chunk of the rich, fluffy concoction into his mouth to keep from saying more.

"I want you to know I have no objection to staff dating should the opportunity arise. I do, however, wish they would be discreet."

Lance nearly choked. "I have no intention of dating Elaina but should someone else catch my fancy I promise to be discreet." He took another sample of the scrumptious treat then slid his chair closer to hers. "So, what's your stand on the boss dating?"

The air between them vibrated.

Her face turned a lovely shade of pink. Lance locked his gaze with hers in a heated embrace, put his dessert down, then leaned in closer and cupped her cheek in his palm. He brushed chocolate from the corner of her mouth then traced her lips with his thumb. Her soft sigh of pleasure may as well have been a strong aphrodisiac, given its reaction in him. Before Lance could shorten the distance between them and move in for a kiss, the phone rang.

He bit back a curse. Groaned.

Kyleigh cleared her throat and answered. "Silver Star Ranch, can you hold please?" Placing her hand over the receiver, she gave him a tentative smile. "Thank you for the cake."

His chance over, Lance gathered up his unfinished dessert and carried it with him to the bunkhouse. The delectable confection did nothing to assuage his craving for her. Since Robert had campfire duty, Lance decided to drive into town and grab a beer someplace quiet but all he managed to do was think about Kyleigh and how she'd come to mean a great deal to him in such a short amount of time.

* * * * *

The next few days passed in a flurry of activity as guests came and went. Kyleigh, Ramona, Elaina, and two temporary workers barely kept the food fresh and rooms clean, therefore tensions stayed at an all-time high. Lance, Robert, and a day wrangler had their share of long rides and short tempers, but for the most part, Thanksgiving proved a huge success.

Two days after the final guest checked out, Kyleigh sat in the office catching up on the bookkeeping. Ramona inventoried the kitchen while Robert wrote up an order for feed and hay. Lance checked the horses for loose shoes and stone bruises.

Elaina and Tess, the only other worker who'd stayed on to help with housekeeping, muddled their way through the rooms and laundry.

"So, who's the hunky cowboy belong to?"

Elaina spared the other woman a brief glance. "Robert is Ramona's husband. Lance is spoken for."

"I didn't see a ring."

"Yeah, well, that means nothing."

Tess arched an eyebrow at her. "He yours?"

"Not yet, but he will be, so hands-off if you know what's good for you."

"Is that a threat?"

Elaina shrugged. "I don't make threats, I make promises."

Chapter Five

In the days following Thanksgiving, the Silver Star transformed into a fairytale of lights, elves, and cowboy Santas. Decorated boughs and branches filled every nook and cranny of the buildings and lights draped the trees along the drive. Stockings—one for each employee— hung on the mantle above the huge fireplace in the lodge room. Mistletoe graced the entryways. Not wanting to get caught beneath a sprig, Lance peeked in the window before opening the door, then hurried through.

Although she hadn't actually thrown herself at him again, Elaina still made him nervous when they happened to be in the same space.

Kyleigh's marketing efforts continued to pay off as seldom a day or week went by without at least a few guests. As they had at Thanksgiving, Christmas Eve and Day feasts would begin around 11 a.m. and continue until 6 p.m., followed by a hayride and caroling around the campfire. Today, though, he hoped to convince his boss to take a drive with him.

He hesitated a moment, leaned against the doorjamb and watched her designing ads for the upcoming festivities. Two computer monitors boasted graphics and text made to entice people into choosing to spend Christmas and/or New Year's at the Silver Star. His heart swelled at the talent displayed before him. *She's definitely in her element, and brilliant at what she does.* He waited to knock until after she took a breath and leaned back in her chair. She turned. His pulse skipped a thud at the smile she bestowed on him.

"Can I help you?"

Yeah, run away with me for a wild, passionate weekend. Heat climbed up his neck. Lance reeled in his wayward thoughts and cleared his throat. "I thought we'd take a drive to Lost Maples State Natural Area. I hear it's beautiful, especially this time of year before winter sets in." Before she could hesitate or make excuses he stepped forward and took her hand. "C'mon, we both could use the break. I've already cleared it with Mona and Robert," he added, a grin tugging at his lips.

"Well, looks like I don't have a lot of choice then." The surprise and pleasure in her tone belied the severity of the words.

He reached down and caressed her cheek. "You always have a choice with me, but I'd really like you to come along."

Her quick intake of breath did funny things to his insides. Lance allowed the sharp sweetness of emotions to envelop him.

"OK. I'll change into hiking shoes, grab a jacket, and meet you at the truck."

"Great. I'll see you in a bit."

Lance walked with her to the back door and watched a moment as she hurried to her cabin, then went into the kitchen to retrieve the picnic lunch he'd asked Ramona to prepare for them.

"She agreed to go?"

He nodded.

Mona's sigh reverberated through the room. "Good. I'm glad." She hesitated, eyed him a moment. "You'll be good for her and to her. Won't you?"

Lance hugged her. "Count on it."

Elaina walked into the kitchen just as the quick embrace ended. "Well, this is interesting...."

Lance ground his teeth. "Get your mind out of the gutter, Elaina, she's a married woman."

"Yeah, and I wonder what her *husband* would think if he'd walked in on you instead of me."

Ramona straightened her shoulders and faced Elaina squarely. "That I was hugging a friend. Robert's had my heart for more than ten years now and has no reason to doubt my feelings or loyalty. But just in case you're thinking of testing that, I'd suggest you reconsider."

Lance stepped toward Elaina. "You need to grow up, little girl."

Before anyone could say more, Kyleigh entered through the laundry room, a sketchpad tucked under her arm. "I thought we were going to meet at the truck?"

Lance backed away from Elaina and picked up the bag of food, then turned to Kyleigh with a smile he far from felt. "Sorry, got sidetracked. Let's go."

Tension followed them like a noxious cloud. Once they passed through the Star's gate, Kyleigh touched his arm. "Was something going on with Elaina I need to know about?"

Lance blew out a frustrated breath. "She's such a brat. Her very presence keeps me on edge. I can't afford any trouble with or from her."

"She thinks she's in love with you."

He snorted. "The only thing Elaina is in love with is Elaina and her ideals and dreams."

"I don't think that's quite true." Kyleigh's soft voice held a hint of chastisement. "I think she's a young woman who's either too used to getting her way or has had to fight for everything she's ever wanted in life. And, right now, that's you."

"So, what do we do about her?"

"We?"

He grinned. "Yeah, we. You hired the woman, therefore you have to help me deal with her."

Her giggle chased away the lingering annoyance.

Every mile of the trip from the ranch, located just outside of Kerrville, to Vanderpool bespoke the vast beauty of the Hill Country. Even in early December, wildlife dotted pastures of rich green. Golden hues of sand and limestone jutted into the blue sky and multi-colored foliage covered hills and canyons and set the horizon ablaze.

Lance maneuvered his SUV around the bends and across the peaks and dips with ease. The sleek vehicle hugged curves the way a lover would a beautiful woman. He'd never considered himself an adrenaline junkie, but 'Rocky Mountain High' didn't hold a candle to the thrill coursing through his veins on this gorgeous drive with Kyleigh beside him. Sunrays highlighted the rich auburn curls she'd tucked into a sleek ponytail. Her eyes, alight with sensitivity, combined with a wicked sense of humor, increased his awareness to unbearable heights and filled the cab with fun and laughter.

They stopped for coffee in Bandera then continued toward their destination. In a spur-of-the-moment decision, Lance turned the opposite direction of the park.

"Where are we going?"

"Utopia. A surprise visit to an old employer. I think you'll love it."

Kyleigh remained silent until he pulled into the gate of the Crossed Penn ranch. The winding road, colorful flora and majestic hills leading up to and surrounding the huge lodge and area housing caused her breath to catch in an audible hiss. "My word, we're small potatoes compared to this! Why did you leave?"

He laughed. "I'm not a huge fan of crowds. Especially the creative types. The Crossed Penn is an exclusive artists retreat. Anne and Bill Penn represent people from all over the country. And they're always packed." He opened the door, disembarked, and walked around to help her out. "Bring your sketchpad."

"I will not. These are professionals and that's presumptuous!"

Lance reached around her and grabbed it himself. "No, Kyleigh, it's not. They're as down-home as you can get and genuinely appreciate art in every form." He put a finger over her lips to stop her protests then held out his hand. She huffed a breath, slipped her palm into his, and gripped it nervously. He lifted her knuckles to his mouth. "Trust me, Anne will love looking at your work."

Within minutes of walking through the huge, oak door, they were met with squeals of delight from a small woman of Native American heritage. She put both hands on his shoulders and kissed each cheek. "Lance, darling. How are you?"

He let go of Kyleigh's hand and returned her embrace. "I'm wonderful. How's Bill and the gang?"

"Everyone's fine. Recuperating from the Fall Festival. Don't be rude, darling. Introduce me to your friend."

Lance turned and pulled Kyleigh close. "Kyleigh Winters, meet Anne Penn. Kyleigh owns a small guest ranch outside Fredericksburg. We're on our way to Lost Maples and decided to take a slight detour to see how y'all are getting on."

Anne embraced Kyleigh in the same manner she had Lance. "So nice to meet you, darling," she said then glanced back at him. "You've stopped roaming, have you?"

Her uncanny intuition had always unnerved him. Lance nodded.

"Well, you've got yourself a prize with this one," she told Kyleigh. "Lance here was one of the best ranch hands we've ever employed. We were sorry to lose him in such a short time."

"How long did you work here?" Kyleigh asked.

Anne's chuckle drew Kyleigh's attention back to her before he could answer. "I think he stayed, what.... a week? Two?"

Lance rolled his eyes, grinned. "Felt more like a year."

Laughter rang from the woman's throat in a melodious tinkle. "Do you like art, Kyleigh?"

"She's an artist herself," Lance interjected before Kyleigh could answer.

Kyleigh flushed. "I dabble some, but yes, I love art. Lance says you've some wonderful exhibits here."

"He's correct. Would you like a tour?"

"If you have time."

"We always make time for guests and friends." She slipped her arm through Kyleigh's and led them deeper into the lodge.

The tour took less than an hour. Before they left, Lance pulled out his cell phone and showed Anne the pictures he'd taken of Kyleigh's paintings, then handed her the sketchbook. The hums of appreciation and delight she expressed while perusing the tablet filled him with a ridiculous amount of pride.

"Beautiful stuff. If you ever decide to expand your inventory or have a showing, give me a call."

Kyleigh thanked her but didn't say a whole lot during the thirty-minute drive into the park. Lance wondered if he'd overstepped his boundaries.

The five-plus mile trek through the forest of big tooth maples, across the streams, and up the canyon provided ample opportunity to hold her hand or put an arm around her waist when crossing a slick rock or navigating slippery terrain. Upon reaching the highest point on the trail, Lance brushed leaves off a huge, flat rock, set his backpack down, and turned her in his arms. "You've been awfully quiet since we left the Crossed Penn. You're not angry or upset with me about showing Anne your work, are you?"

"A little shell-shocked, but not angry. I never thought of my painting as anything other than a personal pleasure and a way to gift others. Anne was very generous to offer the opportunity for it to be more."

"Definitely something to think about," Lance said as he unpacked their lunch.

They enjoyed a comfortable quiet time as they feasted on the thick ham and cheese sandwiches, fresh fruit, and iced tea Ramona had provided.

"Whew! Not sure if I'll be able to get back down after all that," Kyleigh said with a laugh.

Lance chuckled. "Aren't you glad you came?"

"I am. This place is beautiful. So serene."

He'd been trained to read people—expressions and body language. The relaxed pose in which she rested encouraged him to close the minute distance between them. He cradled her head in his palm and lowered his mouth toward hers. "You're what's most beautiful about this whole day."

A shiver trembled through her. One he responded to on a visceral level. He edged closer. Kyleigh placed a hand against his chest, then lifted her lips to his. Though brief, the kiss held all the promise of tomorrow. Lance cuddled her against his shoulder and sank his hands into her hair, shaking it loose, until it rippled across her back in luxurious waves. Awe and gratitude filled his soul. For the first time in his life, he allowed himself to believe in the possibilities love had to offer.

* * * * *

Elaina sat on the edge of her bed, her face buried in the pillow clasped tight against her chest. Tears streamed down her cheeks. Sobs wracked her frame. Watching Kyleigh leave with Lance this morning had been the final straw that broke the tenuous hold she had on the hope for a better life. She rocked back and forth, as her heart shattered into tiny shards, searing the breath from her body.

Why, oh why has any man I've ever loved not given a rat's ass about me?

"Elaina. I love you."

The voice stopped her frantic movements. Goosebumps pimpled her flesh. She whispered into the stillness.... "Who are you?"

"I am the *One* who calls you by name and loves you unconditionally."

Fearing she was losing her grip on reality just as her mother had, Elaina lunged off the bed and fled the room. Running off the porch, she dropped to her knees, scrambled up, and continued her mad dash down the drive. Stumbling over the rocks that lined the road, she tripped and fell. Grit and gravel embedded into her palms.

Brakes squealed. A horn blared. Lights blinded her.

Elaina screamed as heat and dust gushed from beneath the wheels that stopped inches from her face.

"Elaina!" Kyleigh bolted from the SUV, grabbed her by the shoulders, and helped her to her feet. "Are you all right?"

She trembled so hard her teeth chattered. "Th-there's a m-man i-in-the-bunkhouse."

Lance appeared from the other side of the vehicle. "Where? Can you describe him?"

She shook her head. "Just...heard him talking."

"Talking to whom?"

She shrugged, not about to admit the voice spoke to *her*.

"C'mon, let's get you back to the house."

"N-not the bunkhouse. P-please."

"The lodge then," Kyleigh said.

Elaina accepted their help into the truck, then moved over, grateful when Kyleigh climbed in beside her and wrapped her in a firm embrace. Within moments they were parked at the lodge.

Lance opened the vehicle door. Kyleigh helped Elaina down and inside. Alerted by the bell on the lodge door, Robert and Ramona hurried into the room.

"Get her something to drink, Mona, while your mother cleans and bandages her hands. Robert, come with me."

No one questioned, just rushed to do Lance's bidding.

He and Robert combed the area inside and out and several yards in each direction surrounding the large mobile home that had been converted to two smaller residential suites. Twenty minutes later they returned to the lodge.

"Nothing," Lance replied to the question in their eyes. "Not a footprint. No evidence of someone trying to get in. Nothing's been disturbed inside or out. Are you *sure* you heard a man's voice?"

Blood drained from Elaina's face at the doubt and disbelief in his tone. She stiffened and lifted her chin a notch, though her lip trembled. "I know what I heard."

"You been drinking? Doing drugs?"

Footsteps halted Lance's questions. They turned as a young man, the mirror image of Lance himself, approached. Lance's face turned whiter than the bandages on Elaina's hands. "Seth. What are you doing here?"

"Wanted to surprise you, Dad. Looks like I succeeded. Why are you harassing the girl? Can't you see she's terrified?

Chapter Six

Lance stared at his son a moment, then pulled his scattered emotions into a tight ball that lodged in his stomach. He cleared his throat and looked back to Elaina. "He's right. I'm sorry. Didn't mean to harass you. Are you OK?"

Elaina sent Seth a quick, grateful glance. "I'll be fine. Thank you."

"Seth and I will be in my side of the house tonight so if you see or hear anything, just give us a holler."

"Not going to introduce me first?"

"Of course." Lance shot him a tight, rueful smile, then faced the others, waving in their direction as he named each. "Kyleigh, Robert, Mona, my son, Seth. And our damsel in distress here is Miss Elaina."

Murmurs of 'hello' and 'welcome' echoed in the room as Seth shook each person's hand. Elaina's, he lifted to his lips with a smile and whispered, "Pleasure to meet you."

Once introductions were made followed by awkward silence, Lance addressed Seth once more. "Where'd you park?"

Lance pointed to the side entrance. "I'm out that door."

"Let's get your gear and you can ride with me up to the bunkhouse. We'll move your vehicle tomorrow."

"What about Elaina? We're not going to leave her to walk up there alone, are we?"

Lance looked to Kyleigh for direction. *Help me here....*

As though reading his thoughts, she stepped forward and placed a gentle hand on Elaina's shoulder. "You're welcome to stay with me tonight or we can walk with you to the bunkhouse."

Relief flashed over Elaina's face. "I'd rather stay with you if you're sure you don't mind."

Kyleigh smiled. "Not at all. I wouldn't have offered if I minded. Let's go get your gown or pajamas and clean clothes for tomorrow. I'm sure everything will look different in the bright light of morning."

"We'll walk with you," Mona and Robert offered, and fell into step with the two women, leaving Lance and Seth alone.

"Are you in some kind of trouble?"

Seth shifted on his feet and avoided eye contact. Lance heaved a sigh. "Just what I thought. What is it this time?"

"Nothing really. Lost my job. Couldn't pay rent or utilities. Landlords tend to frown on people homesteading their property. So does the law."

"I could have easily sent you some money."

"You don't want me here?"

The baleful look the boy bestowed on him had long stopped affecting Lance the way it used to, back when he felt guilty for everything Seth's mother accused him of, warranted or not. "That's not what I said. I'm just surprised you're here is all."

"Thought I'd try for a fresh start away from Iowa. Someplace warmer."

Pamela S Thibodeaux

"OK, I'll see if Kyleigh can find work for you. If not, I'm sure you can find some around here soon. Lots of places hire seasonal help. We'll get you back on your feet in no time."

Lance knew by the roll of his son's eyes and his long-suffering sigh, Seth wasn't too happy about his plan. Boy seemed to have a problem with responsibility. But he was done supporting a grown man and bailing him out of one scrape after another. He suppressed a grin. "No thanks necessary. Now get your gear and meet me back in here. I want to make a pass through the lodge to be sure no unwanted guests are wandering around."

"You seriously think Elaina made up the story of hearing someone?"

Lance shrugged but refrained from saying what he really thought of Elaina.

"She seemed pretty frightened."

"Maybe. Let's just say I don't trust her implicitly."

"But you're going to check, anyway?"

Lance chose to ignore the quick flash of negative emotion the trace of humor in his son's voice evoked. "Can't be too careful. Mona sometimes comes down pretty early. Kyleigh too."

"Ah, so that's the way the wind blows."

By the sarcasm of his son's voice, something in his own tone must've alerted Seth to his attraction for Kyleigh. Lance swallowed the growl rumbling in his throat. "Mind yourself, Seth. If I see anything less than total respect for either of them—or Elaina for that matter, I'll run you off myself."

"And with a shotgun, no doubt."

This he couldn't let pass. He was damn tired of defending his military career and time of service in the war. He clenched his fists, determined not to react the way Seth obviously wanted him to. "You disrespect *anyone* in my presence, and I promise I won't need a gun of any sort to kick you off this ranch. Now get your gear as I've already told you more than once to do."

With that Lance spun on his heel and stalked up the stairs. In the time he took to check through the corridors and verify the rooms were empty and locked, he decided the walk to the bunkhouse, *after* patrolling the entire perimeter of the house and grounds, would give them both a chance to cool off before sharing the same small enclosure. Back down in the lodge's common area, he and Seth made sure the entrance doors were locked too, then exited through the laundry room.

Lance put sheets on the bed in the spare room, not much bigger than a large closet, and bid his son goodnight. He poured himself a shot of whiskey and carried it with him to his bedroom. After changing clothes, he crawled beneath the covers and savored the smooth drink along with memories of his day with Kyleigh. His dreams that night were of love and laughter and happy-ever-after. Something he hadn't believed in, much less hoped for, in a long time.

* * * * *

The next morning, Kyleigh arrived at the lodge to find Lance already inside and a pot of coffee brewing.

"Morning."

His smile set a horde of butterflies aflutter in her stomach. "Hey. Coffee smells good."

"It'll be ready in a moment. Want me to bring you a cup in the office? Or would you rather sit out here, or maybe on the porch a few minutes before getting started?"

"The porch would be nice. Did Seth get settled in all right?"

"Yeah. I'm sure he'll be down here at some point today. I'd like to talk with you about that, but coffee first. How's Elaina?"

"She seems to be sleeping well. I didn't hear her wandering around after we went to bed."

"Great." He walked over to the cupboard and withdrew them each a mug, poured, then added a pinch of sugar and drop of cream to hers. "Here ya go."

She smiled, sipped. "Thanks. Shall we head outside?"

He nodded and pushed the swinging door open for her, then followed through the common area, past the office and souvenir shop to the huge double-doored entry. She held his coffee while he unlocked those doors then opened one for her to pass through. "Prop it ajar please, so we can hear if someone comes in or the phone rings."

He did as she asked then, once each of them was seated in a rocking chair, Lance took off his hat and raked a hand through his hair. Kyleigh resisted the urge to sink her fingers into the curls at his nape. Her attraction for him scared her as much as it stirred feelings deep in her soul. She had no reason to feel guilty but that didn't stop the sharp stab in her gut. "What did you want to talk about?"

"I wondered if you'd have some work for Seth or if you know someone who might."

"I'm sure we can find something for him to do around here. How long will he be staying?"

"Don't know. He lost his job and, as a result, housing. Not the first time over the last decade or so. Thought he'd try to make a fresh start here. But, Kyleigh, if you think it'll cause problems, I understand if you'd rather him work elsewhere."

"I don't know your son at all, Lance, so it's not me who has to decide that. Do you two get along well enough to work together?"

"There was a time when I'd have said a definite no, but now, I'm not so sure. He hasn't been too dependable, but then again, neither was his mother. Maybe here, he can learn to stand on his own two feet. I'm hoping his seeing Robert and Ramona, who are younger than him, doing so well will give Seth an incentive to grow up."

"He sure seemed to take a shine to Elaina."

"You think so?"

Kyleigh nodded. "His jumping to her defense so quickly without knowing the whole story is a pretty good indication."

Lance's wry smile was slightly mocking. "Doubt it was as much in defense of her as it was a chance to challenge me."

The hint of pain and shame in his voice pricked her heart. "Must be hard to raise a child when you're gone so much."

"Yeah. First the military. Then his mother drove a wedge between us with her lies and accusations and constant moving. I've tried everything I know to show my love and support, especially since he turned eighteen nine, almost ten, years ago, but that time follows me like a bad rap sheet."

"Well, perhaps this will be the beginning of changing all that. Talk with Robert and let him be the boss, so to speak, over Seth. Might make it less tense between the two of you. He can help in the corral and with maintenance. We'll get busier as the holidays approach. After the new year, we'll reevaluate."

"Thanks." Lance finished his coffee, then slid his chair closer to hers. "Great day, yesterday."

"Yes, lovely."

He leaned in, crooked a finger in her blouse, tugged—an unspoken request to shorten the distance between them. Kyleigh tapped a finger on his chest. "Discretion...."

He grinned. "We're not on the clock yet."

Her lips bowed. He nibbled on the corner of her mouth, then laid his over hers in a gentle caress.

The swoosh of the door leading from the kitchen into the lodge followed by footsteps heading in their direction interrupted the moment.

"Later," he whispered and moved away just as Robert called for Kyleigh.

"Out here!"

Robert paused in the doorway, his eyebrow arched in question. "We have any guests checking in today?"

Kyleigh shrugged. "I'll have to check the calendar and website, but I don't think so. Why?"

"Thought we'd get that new trail cleared. You game, Lance?"

"Sure am. If you'll give me half an hour, I'll have us another pair of hands to help with the job."

"Good deal."

Lance left to rouse his son.

Robert took the chair Lance vacated, sipped his coffee, and sighed. "God, I love the sunrise and sunsets here. The way the colors vary and change from dark to light or vice versa and how the light reflects off the hills."

Kyleigh smiled. "Yeah. Even rain clouds rolling across them are lovely in their own way."

"The way thunder echoes across the peaks or lightning slashes through the sky. How's Elaina?"

"She's fine, as far as I know. Where's Mona?"

A frown creased Robert's brow. "She's a little under the weather today. Will you check on her later and radio me if y'all need anything?"

"Of course."

He finished his coffee, stood, and held a hand out to her. "You sure one of us shouldn't stay around the lodge? I'd hate to leave you women alone if someone was wandering around here last night."

Kyleigh accepted his hand-up and rose. She took a deep breath, said a quick, silent prayer, and tuned into her intuition. "Chances are what Elaina heard was a figment of an overactive imagination brought on by the stress of the last few weeks. We'll be fine."

"OK, but keep the radio handy at all times."

"Will do."

"Good deal. I'm going to whip up a quick batch of scrambled eggs and sausage for us before we head out. You hungry?"

Kyleigh hugged her son-in-law. "No, but thanks. I'll get something a little later."

The phone rang and cut off Robert's response. Kyleigh hurried into the office, grabbed her pen, and answered the call.

* * * * *

"Mom?"

Static made hearing difficult. Kyleigh picked up the radio, keyed the mike, and answered her daughter. "I'm here, sweetheart. How do you feel?"

"My stomach is a wreck. Anyone else having issues?"

"Not that I'm aware of."

"Is Elaina in? I don't think I'm going to make it out of the house today."

"I'll go get her and check on you. Be there in a few minutes."

"OK. Thanks."

Kyleigh put a sign on the office door indicating she'd be back in fifteen minutes, locked up, and headed out and up the hill to her house. "Elaina!"

When there was no response, Kyleigh opened the door to her guest room to find the bed neatly made and Elaina nowhere in the cabin. She decided to check on Ramona before walking over to the bunkhouse to see if Elaina was there. She found her daughter in the bathroom, doubled over the commode, wretchedly ill. Grabbing a washcloth, she ran it under cool water, passed the rag over her daughter's face, then filled the cup on the counter. Placing the cloth against her forehead, she urged Mona to rinse her mouth, then helped her into the bedroom to lie down. "How long have you been like this?"

"Since early this morning."

Kyleigh placed the back of her hand against Mona's forehead, then cheeks. "You don't feel feverish. I'm going to get some crackers and a sports drink and leave them by the bed. Eat if you can."

"I'd rather have ginger ale or a soft drink."

"You got it." Kyleigh tucked the covers around Ramona then gathered the items from the kitchen. She rinsed the cloth out with cold water and placed it on the tray, and pulled a trashcan close.

"Here ya go. Holler if you need anything else and I'll be here as quick as I can."

Mona sighed. "Thanks, Mom."

Kyleigh sat with her for a few more minutes, then left when Mona dozed off. She went over to the bunkhouse where she found Elaina and Seth sitting on the porch.

"Good morning, Ms. Kyleigh."

"Hey there. I need you to come in to work today. Mona's not well."

Elaina scrambled to her feet. "I'll finish dressing and be right down."

"Thanks." Kyleigh turned to Seth. "I thought you'd be out with Robert and your dad."

"I begged off for this morning. Need to get a load or two of laundry done and settle in. I'll help them after lunch."

"Sounds fine. We'll need some paperwork from you if you're going to work for us, so come on down to the office. I'll get the employee packet together and you can move your truck while you're at it."

"Yes, ma'am," he said with a slight salute.

Kyleigh couldn't say he intended to mock her but something about the hard look he sent her way set her teeth on edge.

Thirty minutes later he and Elaina walked in together. Kyleigh handed Seth the employee packet with the forms he needed to fill out clipped on top. She then went over the schedule and explained to Elaina the duties she needed to tend to. Once both were busy with the tasks at hand, she radioed Robert to see what time he and Lance would be in for lunch and questioned him as to their preference of food for the meal.

The morning wore on without much incident. When Kyleigh closed the office to cook lunch, Ramona sailed into the kitchen as though she hadn't been sick a day in her life.

"Talk about a quick recovery...."

Mona laughed. "Right! I took a little nap and when I woke up, felt like my old self. So here I am. What's on the agenda?"

"About to grill hamburgers and potatoes for the guys."

"I'll get it. I'm sure you've plenty to do for the upcoming festivities."

Before Kyleigh could respond, the bell on the lodge door rang. She hurried out and spent the next half hour checking in a young family who showed up without reservations. She then gave them a tour of the building and grounds and escorted them to their room.

Lance and Robert rode in from the trails and everyone, including the unexpected guests, sat down to enjoy the food Mona had prepared. After eating, Robert asked Seth to help with the trail clearing then addressed Lance. "If you don't mind, saddle up some horses and take our guests on their ride."

Lance donned his hat, got up from the table and put his dishes away. "It'd be my pleasure. Meet y'all in the corral in thirty minutes."

The family scraped their plates then exited the room with murmurs of excitement. Ramona and Elaina continued the housekeeping and decorating chores while Kyleigh resumed her office, marketing, and advertising duties.

Chapter Seven

For the third day in a row, Ramona, pale and clammy, shook Robert awake.

"What is it?"

"I need the trash can. I'm afraid I won't make it out of bed."

He jumped from beneath the covers, shivered in the cold, and hurried to the bathroom. *I'll be glad when this stomach bug or whatever she has runs its course.* He made sure the can had a new liner and a handful of paper to absorb the contents of Mona's meal from the night before and carried it to her. Once she finished retching, he removed the bag and took it into the laundry room to bring to the dumpster on his way to the lodge. "I'll tell Mom you'll be late again this morning."

Mona moaned her agreement and rolled over onto her side

Robert dressed and decided to eat breakfast at the lodge. The smell of his cooking the past few days seemed to add to his wife's distress. He met Kyleigh on her way to the big house and fell into step beside her. "Mona's sick again this morning."

Kyleigh eyed him. "Funny how she's deathly ill in the mornings and yet, right as rain by noon."

The light in his mother-in-law's eyes and smug smile told Robert she knew something he didn't. "What?"

"Robert, *morning* sickness...."

She laughed when he stumbled due to the lack of blood going to his brain. "Morning.....? Oh! You think...?"

Kyleigh grinned. "I'd bet my last dollar."

He whooped and swung her around. "I'm going to check on her! What should we do?"

Kyleigh chuckled. "If I were you, I'd run to the drugstore and pick up a home pregnancy test. If it comes out as I think it will, she'll need to set an appointment with her OBGYN soon."

"Right. Tell Lance I'll be back in time for the morning trail ride."

"Don't worry, we got 'cha covered."

Two hours later, Robert and Mona entered the lodge arm-in-arm, glowing brighter than the Christmas lights donning every room. "Well, what'll it be? Grandma, Maw Maw, Nana, Neena, or MiMi?"

Kyleigh hugged her daughter. "I'll have to think about that," she said with a laugh. "How are you feeling?"

"Better now that I know the reason behind all this craziness. How long do you think the sickness will last?"

Kyleigh shook her head. "Could be weeks. Could be months. Everyone is different. I had a little queasiness with you the first couple of months, but that was it."

Mona frowned. "Guess I'm reaping what I sowed—multiplied."

Kyleigh laughed again. "You know what they say...you don't pay for your raisin' till you raise one."

"Uh oh," Robert chimed. "Guess I'll be paying for both our raisings then," he teased and swept Mona up into a hug. "I need to catch up with Lance, so holler if you need me."

He bid them adios and cautioned Mona to take it easy.

Kyleigh led Mona into the dining room and had her prop her feet up. "We'll give Elaina more hours and bring Tess on full time so you're not on your feet so much."

Ramona rolled her eyes. "Mom...I'm pregnant, not an invalid. Let's not put me on bed rest just yet."

Kyleigh's cheeks grew warm. "You're right. I'm sorry. But, if I remember correctly, the first few months are the trickiest. Your second trimester should be a breeze, then the last several weeks can get mighty uncomfortable. I don't want you waiting until the last moment to get someone hired and trained."

"If Elaina and Tess can handle mornings as long as this sickness continues, I'll be fine for the other meals."

"Ok. But get the girls or one of the men, or me for that matter, to help you with heavy lifting."

"Yes, ma'am. Shall we tell everyone at lunch?"

Kyleigh smiled. "Yeah, let's."

Mona scooted back from the table. "Great! I'm going to prepare the biggest celebration feast you've ever seen. Well, big enough for the few guests and us, but elegant nonetheless."

"Knock yourself out. Figuratively speaking of course. Congratulations, darling," Kyleigh murmured when Mona laughed and hugged her. When her daughter headed toward the kitchen, Kyleigh bowed her head and swallowed a sob. *Oh, Dennis...you're missing so much....*

His voice rose up from deep within her heart. "No, darling, I'm not. I held our little one before sending it on to bless you all."

Guess you won't tell me what 'it' is.

Kyleigh smiled when his chuckle resounded in her mind. "Now, where would be the fun in that?"

Whispering her love and sending a kiss heavenward, Kyleigh went into the office and put a call in to Tess to see if she wanted the extra work.

"Oh, yes, Ms. Kyleigh! I'd love to work more hours. As long as Elaina doesn't mind."

"What does Elaina have to do with your decision?"

Tess stuttered, then grew quiet. "I don't want to get her in trouble. She was just a little miffed at me the last day I was there after Thanksgiving."

"What about?"

"Lance."

Kyleigh's hackles rose at the thought of the two younger women arguing over him. "Well, I believe that situation is resolved. Lance isn't interested in a relationship with Elaina."

"Oh?"

The hope in Tess's voice grated on Kyleigh's last nerve. She counted backward from five and huffed a frustrated breath. "So, can we count on you to be here in the mornings, or should I give someone else a call?"

"I'll be there. Thanks!"

"Great. See you tomorrow." Kyleigh hung up the phone praying she wasn't making the biggest mistake of her life by bringing another woman panting after Lance into the fray.

Later, after plates were filled and all were seated at the table for the noon meal, Kyleigh raised her glass. "I'd like to propose a toast."

Glasses lifted in anticipation of her words.

"To my lovely daughter and wonderful son-in-love. Children are the most precious treasures you'll ever find. The greatest gift you'll ever receive. The most challenging career you'll ever have and the purest joy you'll ever know. Ramona and Robert, may God bless and keep you and yours in the palm of His mighty hand. May He grant you peaceful nights, precious memories, and joy unspeakable. Parenting is the biggest challenge and the most rewarding endeavor you'll ever experience. And to my beautiful grandbaby...may the Lord's hand cradle and protect you as you are fearfully and wonderfully knitted together. May you grow and develop without complications and your birth be a safe passage from your mother's womb into our arms."

"Oh.... Mom..." Tears streamed down Mona's cheeks as she clinked glasses with her mother.

Lunch was a lively affair. Everyone laughed and talked and tossed out baby names. Afterward, Kyleigh called Elaina into the office.

"I've hired Tess to help with breakfast shift and housecleaning."

Elaina fidgeted.

"Is there a problem?"

She shook her head. "No, ma'am. We didn't see eye to eye on a couple of things when Tess last worked, but I'm sure that's not a problem now."

"Yeah, she mentioned you were miffed at her about something. Well, some*one*."

Elaina flushed and avoided Kyleigh's gaze. "That was when I thought there might be something between me and Lance. I'm over that now."

Kyleigh arched a brow at her. "Really?"

"Yes. I thought about what all you said, and I realized he is too old for me."

"I'm glad to hear that. So, there won't be a problem between you and Tess then, will there?"

"Not on my part."

Kyleigh acknowledged Elaina's comment with a nod. "Good. She'll be here in the morning. I'll rework the schedules for next week but for now, help Mona as much as you can and, Elaina, please don't let her pick up anything."

Elaina smiled. "I won't. I remember when my mom was expecting my little brother. She could hardly get out of bed. But again, she was always sickly, even when not pregnant. She lost the baby a few weeks after finding he was a boy."

"I'm sorry to hear that. How is she now?"

Sadness clouded the young woman's face. "She's not too well. She's in a mental hospital. I haven't seen her in a while."

Heartbroken at the girl's admission and yet glad she felt comfortable enough to share. Kyleigh embraced Elaina. "Well, if you want to take some time off to go see her, we will work that out."

"Thank you, but I don't."

"How old were you, Elaina, when she went into the hospital?"

"Fifteen."

"Goodness! And your father?"

Elaina shrugged. "Don't know who he is or where he's from. For a while, it was just me and my older brother, Jim, but he died of an overdose a few years ago. It's just me now."

Kyleigh drew the girl into a hug. "You're not alone, Elaina, not as long as you're with us."

"Thank you, Ms. Kyleigh. I appreciate that."

* * * * *

Lance finished up in the corral and set the horses loose for the night, then fed and groomed Champ. The chore soothed him as much as the animal after a long day, but now he wanted a hot shower and a cold beer. He paused on the stoop when a giggle, followed by Seth's hearty laugh, rang out from Elaina's side of the bunkhouse. Before he could decide whether to order him home or leave them be, her door opened.

Seth stepped out. "Hey, Dad. We're just about to head into town for a cold one and some supper. Want to join us?"

The change in his son's demeanor in the week or so since he showed up surprised, and pleased, Lance. "Where are y'all going?"

Seth shrugged. "Haven't decided yet."

"Anywhere but Mexican food," Elaina inserted, stepping out and clicking the door shut.

Lance grinned. "What's wrong with Mexican?"

"Nothing, but I'm hungry for a big ol' steak. Can't get a good steak in a place that sells fajitas."

He chuckled. "Got a point there. Think I'll pass. I'm ready to get these boots off and sit awhile on something that doesn't fret beneath me. Thanks for the invite, though."

"Can we bring you something back?" Elaina offered.

"Nah, I'll grab something here. You two have fun and be careful. Deer are out all over the place with this clear weather and full moon."

"We will." The young folks jumped down the steps and climbed into the truck.

Lance waited until Seth backed out of the drive, then went into the house. One at a time, he hooked a heel in the jack and removed his boots. He took a deep breath, stretched, and decided the shower could wait. Unsnapping his shirt, he got a whiff of his own scent. *On second thought....*

He tucked a beer into the ice bucket in the freezer, grabbed another from the fridge, unscrewed the top and took a swig, then made his way to the bathroom. The hot water and steam did wonders for his aching back and shoulders.

"Lance!" A high-pitched, feminine voice called from the living room.

Damn, forgot to lock the door. "Be out in a minute!" he answered, wondering who would be so bold as to enter without his express permission. He wrapped a towel around his waist, slipped into the bedroom, and struggled into jeans. Before he could don a shirt, the door opened.

"It's just me, Cowboy. You need some help?"

He spun around and stepped away when Tess reached for him. Anger spewed between clenched teeth. "I need you to get out. Who the hell invited you in here, anyway?"

Tess stumbled back, her eyes wide and innocent. "I thought you said to come on in."

"I said I'd be out in a minute."

Her cheeks flamed but she stood her ground and looked up at him with those puppy-dog eyes, a slight pout to her full lips. "Sorry I misunderstood, but since I'm here...."

The suggestive purr in her voice raised his hackles. Lance's eyes narrowed into tiny slits; teeth ground so hard it's a wonder he didn't spit dust when he spoke. "Apology accepted. Now go."

She flounced away. Lance heard the door slam and her footsteps retreating and collapsed onto his bed. Five minutes later a knock announced another visitor. Slipping a T-shirt on, he finger-combed his hair and strode into the living room, glad when whoever knocked this time, waited for him to answer. He flung the door open, surprised to find Kyleigh rocking in the chair on his porch. A concerned frown creased her brow.

"I saw Tess leaving in a hurry. She seemed somewhat flustered. Everything OK?"

"Misunderstanding on her part. I don't know where these young women get off being so brash."

"Meaning?"

He dragged a hand over his face. "Beer's getting warm. You want one?"

Kyleigh shook her head.

"You want to come in?"

"No. I'll wait here. It's such a lovely evening."

"OK. I'll be back in a minute." He went into the kitchen and took out the beer he'd stashed in the freezer, opened it, guzzled. He slid another in its place, then joined Kyleigh on the porch. "So, to what do I owe the pleasure of you sitting in my chair, sweet Kyleigh? Or is this a professional visit?"

"I saw Tess run out like the house was on fire and just wanted to be sure all is well."

"Get one female fatale off my tail and you hire another," he muttered into the bottleneck before upending the beer once more.

"What happened? Or do I even want to know?"

"She waltzed in here like she had a right to and all but jumped me fresh out of the shower."

Lance placed the bottle against his lips to keep from grinning when anger flashed in her eyes like lightning off the surface of a rough-cut onyx.

"Looks like I'll have to have a talk with her just as I did Elaina. Where is that one, by the way?"

"Out to dinner with Seth."

"Oh?"

"Yeah, they seem to have hit it off well. Guess you were right about that."

"I hope they don't rush into anything. She carries quite a bit of emotional baggage."

"Don't we all," he mumbled, then stood. "Sure you don't want a beer or a glass of wine?"

Kyleigh shook her head.

"How 'bout a bite of supper?"

"No, thanks. I ate with the kids before leaving the lodge. Guess I'll head on home now so you can enjoy your evening."

He held out a hand, wrapped her smaller one in a firm grasp when she accepted, then pulled her out of the chair with a gentle tug. Lifting her fingertips, he gently brushed them against his lips then caressed each with his mouth. "I'll enjoy my evening much more if you stay with me a while," he murmured between nips and kisses.

Her sharp intake of breath did wonders for his ego.

"Why don't you let me heat up leftovers from dinner at the lodge or at my place?"

"Because you're here now and my body is in severe protest of putting boots on again, much less walking anywhere."

She smiled, and his heart skipped a thud. "In that case, a glass of wine would be nice—but only if you let me sip it while I cook, and you take it easy."

Lance opened the door and allowed her to enter before him. "You've got yourself a deal." He stretched out in one chair, feet propped on another, while she puttered around the kitchen and threw together a quick but simple and filling meal. She placed the plate in front of him.

"What would you like to drink?"

"Beer's in the freezer," he answered and dove into the food with gusto. Flavor burst on his tongue at the first bite of seasoned meatballs and potatoes sautéed together with thick gravy served over a heap of rice with a side of pork-n-beans.

They chatted while he ate. Kyleigh told him about her conversation with Elaina and how the young woman was alone in the world. Lance got up and placed his dishes in the sink. "Poor kid. Guess you were right about her having to fight for what she wants out of life, too. Thought I was a pretty good judge of character, but you put me to shame."

"Oh, I doubt that. Not in every instance, at least. But there's something about Elaina that makes me think of a lost child."

"She say any more about hearing voices?"

"No. I wonder if she heard Seth moving around?"

"I asked him about that, but he says he'd just pulled up and come in while we were in the lodge. He hadn't had a chance to walk around or anything. Probably an over-active imagination on her part."

"Guess we'll never know."

Lance stopped her when she got up and moved toward the sink. "Leave 'em. You cooked; I'll clean."

"Fine. Dessert and coffee on the porch?"

"I have dessert in there?" he asked as the aroma of fresh coffee permeated the air and the robust liquid filled the small pot.

She laughed, gathered cups, poured. "No-bake cookies."

"I wondered what you were doing with those ingredients spread out all over my counter. Sounds great."

Kyleigh handed him the cups, pulled the tray out of the freezer, and tested the consistency of the treats. "They'll be tastier after they've chilled a while but will hit the spot now."

She placed a few on a saucer and followed him out onto the porch.

Lance bit into a snack, hummed with pleasure as the mixture of oatmeal, peanut butter and chocolate melted in his mouth. "So, you had a good day?"

"Yes. Our guests have all gone. Unless someone pops in, we're free for the next few days."

"Wonderful news about the baby yesterday. And that toast was beautiful. You're very talented in more ways than one, sweet Kyleigh."

A lovely flush filled her cheeks. She emitted a self-conscious little laugh. "I have my moments, I guess."

Lance chuckled. "Don't be so modest. You're amazing. As are these." He lifted another cookie in salute.

She giggled. "You sure I can't do anything for you before I go?"

Yeah, you can marry me and fill my life with your love and light. Lance shoved the remainder of the dessert into his mouth to keep the words from bursting through and shook his head. "Thanks," he mumbled around the food.

Kyleigh stood and placed her cup next to his on the small table between them. His heart turned over when she brushed her knuckles along his jaw, then feathered her fingers through his hair. Warmth permeated his entire being from the tender gesture. He captured her hand with his, moved it around to his mouth, and kissed the palm. She curled her hand into a fist and stepped off the porch.

"I'll leave you to it, then." She headed toward her cabin then twirled around, blew him a kiss, and bid him good evening with a smile that lit her entire countenance.

Lance finished his coffee, picked up their dishes and went in to clean his kitchen. Seth and Elaina still weren't home when he crawled into bed and turned on the television.

Chapter Eight

Three nights after their last evening out, Elaina lay on her bed, head spinning with dreams, heart dancing within her breast. *Seth is so sweet! So much like Lance and yet...not. In looks they were almost identical. Except for the eyes.* Seth's were green and softer, kinder, than Lance's dark brown ones.

He'd only been at the ranch a few weeks, but she and Seth spent every spare moment together. *Is this what true love feels like?*

Thoughts rose to taunt her, drowning out the sweetness.... No such thing as true love. You ought to know that by now. Nothing ever lasts. Not your mother. Not your brothers. What makes you think you deserve true love, anyway?

"Because I'm a good person." She spoke into the darkened room. "Sure, I've made mistakes, but underneath I'm a good person. Please, God, give me another chance."

Harsh laughter erupted in her ears. "God? What's He got to do with anything? What makes you think He cares?"

"I do care, Elaina. If only you believe." Quiet authority echoed in those words.

"Who are you?" she whispered, afraid to believe. Scared to hope God had heard her. And terrified she was more like her mother than she cared to admit.

"I am He who loves you with an everlasting love."

A cloud passed over the moon, splayed shadows on her wall. Elaina jumped up and turned on the light. The bulb flashed then popped. Spooked now, she lit a candle to dispel the darkness. Too scared to venture into the shadowy house, she promised herself she'd change the bulb first thing in the morning. She awoke hours later to a room full of smoke and someone banging on her window. Coughing and choking, she stumbled from the room just as Seth busted through the front door.

"Elaina! Oh, my God, are you alright?"

Lance barreled in behind his son and rushed into the bedroom to extinguish flames that had spread to engulf the dresser and most of one wall.

"I—I don't know what happened."

"You fell asleep with a candle burning, that's what."

The anger in Lance's voice slashed what little composure she had. Elaina crumpled into Seth's arms, sobs wracking her frame.

"I.... I'm sorry...I.... d-didn't mean to fall asleep.... Voices...scared me...."

"What voices? What did they say?"

Elaina shook her head and buried deeper into Seth's arms when he admonished his father to stop the interrogation. Before either could say more, Kyleigh, Robert and Ramona rushed into the tiny living room. Questions and answers rang in the air around her, then stillness.

"I-I'm s-sorry, Ms. K-Kyleigh." She took a breath, gathered her scattered emotions, and stood to face them. "I'll pay for the repairs."

Kyleigh hugged her close. "It's all right. We'll talk about that in the morning. You'll come home with me for the rest of the night. Can you grab clean clothes?"

Seth put his arm around Elaina's waist and went with her into the bedroom. They returned shortly with clothes that reeked of smoke.

Kyleigh took the bag from Elaina. "You can sleep in something of mine tonight and we'll throw these in the wash for tomorrow."

"Thank you." She turned to Seth and Lance. "Thank you both. You probably saved my life."

Seth ran a hand down her arm in a soothing gesture. "Get some rest. We'll figure this all out in the morning."

When Elaina and Kyleigh left along with Robert and Ramona, Seth whirled on his father. "Why are you such a jerk toward her?"

"People who hear voices are a danger to themselves and everyone around them. I've lived with them, worked with them, and fought beside them. So trust me...I know."

"Well, this is not the Marines, and she is not a soldier in some stupid war."

"She's been a thorn in my side since the first day Ramona hired her, and I don't trust her, but it's obvious you see something I don't. I'll try harder. Let's get some shut-eye and we'll clean this up tomorrow."

Seth shrugged off the hand his father placed on his shoulder. "You go. I'm staying here. If she's hearing voices, I'm going to find out where they're coming from."

"Fine. Holler if you need me."

Seth sneered. "I haven't *needed* you for years."

Only after Lance left did Seth allow the sharp glint of pain that flashed in his father's eyes to prick his heart. *Guess I'm as big a jerk toward him as he is toward Elaina.*

He rubbed a palm over his chest, chased away the ache. "I'll try harder too, Dad," he whispered, and then set about cleaning up Elaina's bedroom.

* * * * *

Ensconced in her prayer closet, Kyleigh petitioned the Lord on how to help Elaina. For hours after she'd brought her home, the young woman shivered and cried until Kyleigh climbed in the bed and rocked her like she would a child. When Elaina fell into an exhausted slumber, Kyleigh dozed a few hours beside her. She awoke to the girl's whimpering and stroked her hand over Elaina's head in a calming gesture while she hummed a tune.

Once Elaina settled again, Kyleigh slipped from beneath the covers, slid her feet into slippers, and padded her way to the small room adjacent to the one she slept in, which she'd designated for prayer and meditation. She lit a candle and sat, Bible in her lap, and waited for inspiration. *Dear God, Your word is a lamp unto my feet and a light unto my path. Please show me what I need to know. Elaina is Your child, and she is lost and afraid.*

Tiny pinpricks of electricity feathered over her flesh. Scriptures filled her mind.

My sheep hear my voice, and I know them, and they follow me.

Behold, I stand at the door and knock. If anyone hears my voice and opens the door, I will come in to him, and eat with him, and he with me.

And after the earthquake a fire; but the Lord was not in the fire: and after the fire a still small voice.

"It is You, isn't it, Lord, speaking to Elaina?"

"I Am."

"Ms. Kyleigh!" Elaina's frantic voice jerked Kyleigh from her commune with the Lord. She vacated her seat and opened the door.

"I'm here, Elaina," she assured in a soft tone and crawled up beside her once more. "You're safe."

"I was so scared. I know I've made a mess of things and...."

Her words trailed off when Kyleigh shushed her. "Let's not worry about that right now. You need to rest."

Elaina shook her head, pointed at the clock. "I have to be in the kitchen in less than an hour."

"Not a problem. Your clothes are washed, I'll throw them in the dryer and put on a pot of coffee while you take a shower. Then we'll go look at the bunkhouse."

They arrived at the bunkhouse to find Seth, Lance, and Robert assessing the damage.

"How bad is it?" Elaina asked Robert, her eyes wide, face pale.

"Nothing a coat of paint won't fix. Seth, here, did a major clean-up job after you two left. The dresser can be refinished. All-in-all, I'd say we're lucky."

"Luck has nothing to do with it," Kyleigh corrected. "We're blessed." She turned to Elaina. "God had His hand all over you, last night. I believe it is He who is speaking to you."

A kaleidoscope of emotions flittered across Elaina's face. Doubt and unbelief to hope, then despair. "Why would God want to speak to me? I'm nothing. A nobody from nowhere with no one. My mother is a nut case, my brother overdosed. I don't even know who my father is. What would God want with me? And, if it was Him, who was the other voice reminding me how no good I am?"

One by one the men excused themselves until only Kyleigh and Elaina remained. "The Bible calls the devil the 'accuser of the brethren.' If you heard a voice trying to convince you that you're not good enough for God, it was Satan, the father of lies, saying those things."

Elaina rubbed her arms as though chilled. "So, you really think God is speaking to me? That's strange and scary."

Kyleigh hugged Elaina and turned to lead her to the lodge so they could prepare breakfast for the few guests and staff. "It's not strange at all. Do you have a Bible?"

"No, ma'am."

"Our first order of business then is to get you one so you can find out for yourself how God speaks to His children."

"But what if I'm not one of His? I've never had a real relationship with God. My mother talked of Him often and I went to Sunday School as a child, but then life took over and all that stopped."

"As it does with most people," Kyleigh assured. "But that doesn't mean you can't have a relationship with Him. If He is calling to you, it's because He wants you back into His fold."

Their conversation didn't cease while the two cooked breakfast. "What does He sound like?"

Kyleigh stopped mixing pancake batter. "God's voice is always gentle and kind and encouraging."

"Does He call you by name?"

The love she harbored for her Lord welled in Kyleigh's breast, bubbled out. "Oh, yes. And it is so sweet when He does."

The awe on Elaina's face warmed Kyleigh's heart. "I heard Him. He said, 'I love you, Elaina, with an everlasting love.' That was God, wasn't it?"

Kyleigh flipped the flapjacks and beamed over at her. "Yes, sweetheart, that was God. Now let's get this food out before we have a riot on our hands, and then I need to run up and see about Mona."

They hauled food out to the buffet and served the guests. Robert, Lance, and Seth joined them to participate in the fare. Before Kyleigh could go check on her, Ramona sauntered into the dining area looking hardy and robust.

"This smells delicious, Mom. I'm starving!" She dished up a plate and sat next to her husband, then turned to Elaina. "I'm glad you're OK this morning. Robert said the damage is minimal, so we'll have you back in your bed before this day is over."

Elaina flushed. "Thanks. I appreciate everything you're doing for me."

Lance shoved away from the table, slapped his hat onto his head. "If you'll excuse me, I'll get these guests out for their ride." He picked up his dishes, dropped them into the bin, and strolled out.

Robert finished eating and followed in Lance's wake.

Seth addressed Kyleigh. "Is there paint around here or do I need to go into town and pick some up?"

"Take Elaina with you after breakfast is done." She smiled at Elaina. "Pick whatever color you want. Within reason, of course. Since we have to repaint, might as well be a color you like."

Kyleigh lifted a brow at the questioning look on her daughter's face when Seth and Elaina finished their meal and hurried off to clean the kitchen. "What?"

"Something's different in the way you treat her. What happened?"

"God is using this place, and us, to bring her back to Him," Kyleigh answered, then related her prayer time and Elaina's conversation to her daughter. "Your father told me this ranch is my purpose. Now I see God's hand in it and His plan behind it."

"That's great, Mom. I'm glad you're finding meaning and purpose here. Was it just me or did Lance seem a little off?"

"I think he's still a little miffed over the whole incident. I'm sure he'll get over it, but I guess time will tell." She tried to sound positive and confident, but Kyleigh worried over Lance's demeanor and the fact that he was the first to leave Elaina's room earlier when the conversation turned to God.

* * * * *

Lance sat on his horse atop the highest hill the ranch boasted. Christmas was less than a week away and they were free of scheduled guests until then, but they never knew when someone would pop in and want to stay. Seth and Elaina had painted her bedroom and he'd refinished the dresser, hiding the ugly scars left by flames with fresh color. He'd trimmed it out with an intricate geometric pattern stenciled in various shades that picked up the muted hues of her new bedspread and curtains. The work his son was capable of surprised and pleased Lance.

If only he could relate that to the boy.

Kyleigh had lavished praise on Seth, saying she wished he'd been involved in the renovations they'd endured before opening the ranch to the public. She then promised to find more woodwork for him to do for as long as he chose to remain in her employ. The three of them had been thick as thieves ever since.

And that was a problem.

He hadn't had a moment alone with Kyleigh in days. *Time to remedy that.*

Lance whirled his horse around, picked his way down the trail and into the corral. He unsaddled and groomed the animal. After giving Champ an extra helping of oats, he turned the big chestnut loose to roam with the herd, and then ambled to the bunkhouse to shower and dress. Convincing Kyleigh to have dinner with him in town might be easier if he smelled less like a cowboy and more like a gentleman. He cornered her in the office as she tallied up the day's books and prepared a deposit. "Just the lady I wanted to see."

She glanced up, smiled, and his heart stuttered in his chest. "You clean up nice."

Lance chuckled. "Got a hot date."

Her eyebrow arched in question. "Is that a fact?"

He stepped closer, framed her face with his hands. "That's a fact, ma'am. What're you hungry for?"

"What makes you think I don't already have plans for this evening?"

The flush on her cheeks, light in her eyes, and softly curved lips assured Lance she didn't, but he played along for the simple joy the teasing brought. "Cancel them. Nothing is as important as dinner tonight. With me. Just the two of us...wine, food, dancing. No ranch, no kids, no responsibilities."

"A bit demanding, aren't you?"

He took her hands, pulled her to her feet. "That, my lady, was a request. This is a demand," he murmured, then captured her mouth in a hot, hungry gesture. By the time he let her catch her breath again, she was plastered against him, her fingers fisted in his shirtfront.

"Now, about that dinner...you never did say what you're hungry for."

Kyleigh drew in a shaky breath, clung a moment, then stepped out of his embrace. "Give me a few minutes to freshen up and we'll decide on our way into town."

"Lead the way."

She locked the office behind her and walked with him to her cabin. "Would you like a beer while you wait?"

Lance settled in a recliner, raised the footstool. "That'd be nice, thanks."

Kyleigh unscrewed the top off a long neck, slid it into a full-length koozie, and brought it to him, then went into her bedroom to get ready for the evening. Sitting at her vanity, she stared a long moment at her reflection, trying to gauge her response to his invitation. And that kiss! She looked forward to the idea of dining and dancing with him. Still... *He's such a lovely man, but we really don't know each other very well.*

Despite a little more than three months in her employ, drives in the country, hikes in the hills and numerous conversations, she questioned her growing feelings for Lance. *Is he who You've chosen for me, Lord, or am I just lonely? Can I ever really love anyone the way I loved Dennis? Is it fair to Lance if I can't?*

She fingered the wedding rings hanging from the chain around her neck as they'd been for more than seven years. *Help me know what's right.*

Dennis's voice sounded in her mind. "It's time, Kyleigh. Past time. Be brave, darling, and step out in faith."

She struggled to pull a breath in past the fear clogging her airwaves, released it on a sigh. *God, let this not be a mistake.* With that simple prayer and trembling fingers, she fumbled with the clasp, then removed the necklace. She wrapped the gold bands snugly in her palm for a moment, pressed them to her lips, then opened the top of her jewelry box. She settled the bands in a velvet pouch and chose a multi-colored cross on a silver chain to wear. Rising, she moved to her closet and picked out clean jeans, a V-neck sweater, and fur-lined boots. The gleam in Lance's eyes when she joined him sent delicious sensations prancing up her spine.

He snapped the recliner into place and stood, reaching for her hand. "Forget food."

Kyleigh laughed. "Oh, no, cowboy, you've already promised me dinner and dancing."

"Me and my big mouth," he mumbled.

Later, in the wee hours of the morning, Lance toed his boots off on the porch and carried them to his room, careful to be quiet so as not to wake Seth. Dinner had been a lovely affair. Dancing with Kyleigh? A balm to his soul.

He changed clothes, stretched out, and pulled the quilt over him. Within moments dreams ensnared him in the battle of all battles. The spoils.... his son.

And Kyleigh.

He climbed. He crawled. He ran. Bombs exploded around him, blocked them from his view, hindered the path for him to reach and rescue them. He struggled and called out....

Chapter Nine

Seth bolted from a deep sleep at the sound of pure terror in his father's voice. Kicking free of the covers, he lunged out of bed and hopped on the cold floor. His breath fanned out, wisps of fog in the chilly air. His feet met icy tiles as he darted to Lance's room and halted in the doorway, frozen in fear at the all-too-real struggle his father engaged in while asleep.

Somewhere in the back of his mind, he heard Lance's admonition from years ago.... "Don't touch me. Call from the door or the foot of the bed but don't touch me when I'm asleep. No matter what, Seth. You understand?"

His heart clenched. *I do now, Dad.*

He called Lance's name softly, then louder. When Lance continued to wrestle with the demons in his mind, Seth took a step closer. "Dad! Wake up. You're having a nightmare."

Lance stilled but didn't wake. Seth continued to coax him out of the place of war he'd ventured into. He groaned, relaxed his hold on the blanket clenched against his chest. Turned his head toward Seth's voice.

"Seth?"

"I'm here, Dad. Can I get you something?"

Lance shook his head. "Kyleigh?"

"She's home. Safe."

He seemed to breathe easier at the news. "Where am I? What happened?"

Seth settled beside him. "You're at the Silver Star, in the bunkhouse, in your bed. You had a nightmare."

Lance's sharp inhale told Seth his father was not used to sharing his night terrors with anyone.

"So…. Real." Lance opened his eyes, scraped the wetness off his cheeks, and swiped the sweat from his brow.

Relief swept through Seth when Lance's gaze cleared and focused somewhat.

"I couldn't get to you or her. I couldn't save you." A sob escaped at the admission. "I couldn't save any of them."

Every ounce of anger he'd harbored toward Lance drained from Seth's heart as he pulled his father into his arms and held the weeping man tight against his chest. "I'm sure you tried, Dad, and I can almost guarantee they know how hard you fought to get to them. They understand and forgive. You need to let go and forgive yourself."

Lance wrapped his arms around Seth, held on a moment, then leaned back against the headboard. "Thank you, son. I appreciate you being here. And Seth, I want you to know how proud I am of you. The work you did in Elaina's room is amazing. I never knew you were so talented."

Seth bit back the retorts that sat on his tongue, ready to spear at his father at the slightest inclination. His vow to try harder to understand the man who sired him echoed in his mind. Lance must have seen his struggle because a slight, mocking smile crossed his lips.

"But then, I guess I never had or took the time to get to know the depths of talent latent within my only son. I'm sorry for that, along with a whole host of things it's too late—at night and perhaps in life—to get into right now. Just know that I am."

Seth said a quick, fervent prayer for grace and guidance and took the chance God offered him again to reconcile with his father. "I'm sorry too, Dad, for all the times I didn't try to understand you or your job. And all the things I put you and Mom through. All the things I allowed her to put us through."

This time Lance's smile was full and expressed all the love and hope he felt. Love Seth had shunned for years. Regret pierced his heart.

"Water under the bridge, son, but thank you. Get some rest. We have a long couple of weeks ahead of us."

"Maybe I should drag my mattress in here and camp out on the floor. I really don't want to leave you alone."

"I'm fine now. Honestly. You go on back to bed and get some shut-eye."

Seth hesitated a moment then returned to his room, wondering if there was anything he could do to help heal his father's mental and emotional state.

* * * * *

"Aren't there programs out there for PTSD?" Seth asked.

Lance shrugged. For the past two days, he and his son talked more than they had in a lifetime. Unfortunately, all Seth seemed to want to discuss was *his* mental health. "I've tried numerous therapies. Some have worked better than others. I believe time, faith, and trust are the best remedies. The nightmares aren't as frequent and are much less disturbing than even a year ago. Having you here and us getting a shot at a real relationship is bound to do me a world of good. Major strides toward normalcy."

"I just want you whole, Dad. Promise you'll let me do whatever I can, whenever I can. We've been given a second chance here and I don't want to lose you to a heart attack, or some other unknown ailment linked to your time in the Service."

Lance hugged his son and promised.

They finished feeding and grooming the horses and saddled up those needed for the morning trail ride.

After breakfast, Lance pulled Robert aside. "Hey, man, I know it's short notice, but I need a few hours off this afternoon to do a little Christmas shopping."

Robert rolled his eyes, then slapped Lance on the back, a look of pure pity on his face. "Sorry it's you, but glad it's not me. Take all the time you need, we've got this."

Lance laughed. "Thanks."

For the first time in decades, he actually looked forward to celebrating the holidays. Gift ideas he had in abundance and couldn't wait to get to the mall. *Man, you've really got it bad, or have come a long way, to be actually looking forward to going to the mall.*

Hopefully, the stores wouldn't be too picked over since he'd waited until the last possible minute. As usual.

His first stop was Books, Candles, & More where he found the perfect mug for Tess—simple and impersonal. He browsed a Christian store and picked up a daily devotional and journal for Elaina to aid in her walk with the Lord. It still amazed him how narrow-minded and judgmental he'd been toward her. He remembered a time when he was more open and trusting of people and vowed to resurrect the part of him that had lain dormant—buried beneath years of war, death, and strife—for so long.

Robert and Mona were in for a real surprise: a painting that would work well in any room, especially a nursery. It wouldn't hold a candle to the one Kyleigh was working on—about which he was sworn to secrecy—but from what he'd learned about the couple in his months working for them, he knew they'd love and appreciate the gesture.

Kyleigh's present took a little more time, but he left with a basket filled with things she loved.... The special tea she drank, hand lotion he'd seen on her desk and kitchen counter. A large bottle of the perfume she wore, (to drive him crazy of course). A bottle of her favorite wine, a bag of popcorn and a box of the kind of chocolates she indulged in occasionally, and a lovely heart and cross necklace. *Another six months and it would've been a ring.*

He was a little stumped on what to get Seth until he walked into an art supply store. Though a lot lighter in the pocketbook, he'd enjoyed selecting items for each person on his short list and hoped he'd chosen wisely.

And, lucky for him, everything was gift-wrapped by store staff, saving him a barrelful of misery.

Three days later, Christmas Eve dawned bright and clear. And cold. A front had moved in during the night, adding a layer of icy dampness to the already chilly air. The family that had booked every room on the ranch for a reunion over the holiday weekend opted out of trail rides, choosing instead to sit by the fire in the lodge and indulge in Ramona's specialty hot chocolate, eggnog, and holiday snacks.

Although the family would be cooked for and served separately, day guests would begin arriving at 10:30 a.m. and would continue to come and go through the next day. After the last meal and hayride, the employees and guests gathered for a reading of Jesus' birth from the Gospel of Luke. Only then did the staff eagerly retire to Kyleigh's house to play a game of White Elephant before their actual gift exchange.

Lance and Robert had helped rearrange the furniture in Kyleigh's cabin to make room for all of them. The kitchen table, shoved up against the counter, all but overflowed with food and drinks. The recliner and loveseat in the living room had been moved aside and dining chairs as well as a few folding ones formed a semi-circle in front of the Christmas tree tucked in one corner. Gifts spread out two feet from its base.

"Everyone grab a chair," Kyleigh urged. "Your number is taped to the back. Don't look!" she screeched when Robert tried to peek before choosing his. "That's cheating."

"I should go first since I *am* expecting your grandchild."

Kyleigh patted Mona's shoulder. "Sorry, sweetheart, you know the rules."

"Yeah," Lance winked at Kyleigh "No favorites—otherwise I'd be first."

She sent him a saccharine smile. "You go ahead and believe that."

Once all were standing in front of their chosen seats, each pulled the paper off and exclaimed or grumbled at the number they'd drawn and sat down.

"Ha, I go first anyway," Lance taunted. He held his #1 for all to see, then picked up the box with the corresponding figure.

One by one, they opened the crazily wrapped packages, stole from each other, and bartered until the game ended. Weak from laughter and teasing, he watched Kyleigh stuff paper into a trash bag. "OK, now what? Presents then snacks or vice versa?" she asked.

"Presents," everyone chorused.

"Whose going to play Santa?"

Tess stepped forward when no one else volunteered. "I will." She passed around gifts until each had a pile at their feet, then sat on the floor with hers.

"Since you handed them out, you go first," Kyleigh said.

Tess opened her gift from Elaina and gasped with pleasure then held up a gorgeous turtleneck sweater.

So it went. Each took a turn opening a present and showing off the treasure inside before moving on to the next person until none remained beneath the branches laden with ornaments. Afterward, they mingled between the kitchen and living room, visiting, and eating, until the clock struck eleven. Christmas greetings rang out in the night air as Mona and Robert along with Seth, Elaina, and Tess—who was sleeping on Elaina's couch—left.

Lance tucked Kyleigh's hand in his then raised it to his lips. "I'll help you clean up this mess."

"I appreciate that."

With the two of them working together, the chore took less than half the time it would have taken Kyleigh alone. She stood in the doorway while he shrugged into his jacket. "Thank you for the lovely basket filled with my favorite things."

He stroked her cheek with his fingertips and urged her a step closer. "Thank you for the hatpin. Think I'll put it on my dress Stetson. It's too nice to wear every day. Wouldn't want to risk losing it either."

"Your choice," she replied. "Anything else?" she asked when he hesitated in leaving.

"Only this," he whispered and covered her lips with his. He wrapped his arms around her and hauled her against his chest as the tender gesture quickly turned into something hotter and more intense. He restrained from picking her up and carrying her into the bedroom until his arms shook and breath escaped in jagged pants, then ended the kiss in slow degrees. "Merry Christmas, sweet Kyleigh."

She stepped out of his embrace and ran her fingers through his hair. "Merry Christmas, Lance. I'll see you in the morning."

Chapter Ten

The week between Christmas and New Year's was blessedly quiet. Lance sat with Kyleigh on her porch swing, sipping a glass of the wine he'd bought her for Christmas. The wood-burning chiminea Mona and Robert had given her emanated warmth. Smoke curled through its stack into the star-studded sky.

"Beautiful evening."

His cell phone rang before Lance could respond. "Hey, Ellen. Yeah, Christmas was nice. Different. I'm sure it was difficult. Hold on a sec." He punched the mute button. "We got anybody scheduled in the lodge's upstairs suite?"

"No."

"Mind if I bring a friend and her family out?"

Kyleigh blanched. Shock brightened her dark eyes. "Not at all. How many?"

"Four. Mom and three kids, ages 15, 9, and 4."

"I'll go pencil them in." She stood and left him sitting there, alone and concerned at her reaction.

Lance finished his conversation, satisfied when Ellen accepted his offer to fly her and the children out for New Year's and the rest of their holiday vacation. He called the airline, made reservations, then stepped off the porch and met Kyleigh on her way back from the lodge. "You OK?"

She arched a brow at him. Spots of color replaced the paleness in her cheeks. Anger edged her voice. "I'm fine. When will your friend and her children arrive?"

Her frigid tone along with the emphasis she put on 'friend' surprised him. A closer look revealed a hint of mistrust in her expression. *She's jealous!* Lance slid his arm around her waist to halt her hurried ascent up the steps. "It's my buddy's widow and kids. The one whose funeral I attended a couple months back. Nothing or no one for you to worry about."

"What makes you think I'm worried? We have no exclusive arrangement."

He swallowed the chuckle bubbling in his throat and palmed her cheek, ran his thumb across her lips. "Arrangement or not, the unspoken rule, for me at least, is one babe at a time."

"How gallant of you." She all but snarled at him.

He couldn't hide the laugh this time. He turned her in his arms, held fast when she stiffened against his embrace. "Sweet Kyleigh. There's only room in my heart for one woman and that's you."

His lips covered hers in a kiss designed to banish the doubt in her mind and heart. His hands ran over her back and shoulders in a restless gesture. "Jeeze...Kyleigh...my sweet, sweet Kyleigh."

Lance struggled with the words aching to leap from his throat. He stepped back, framed her face with his hands and waited until she raised a wary gaze to his. "I'm too old, been through and seen too much to play the kind of games teenagers play. I've been a wanderer for years, searching for something, someone to anchor my soul. I found that here and I will never abuse your trust or take what we share for granted."

The intensity in his gaze seared her heart. Kyleigh rested her head against his chest and clung to his hard frame a moment then stepped back and stroked the cheek she'd wanted to slap. "Thank you. I'm sorry for doubting you. It's been so long since I felt anything resembling jealousy it threw me off guard. I am so glad you came through our gate, but Lance, only God can be the true anchor of your soul."

He smiled and brushed his lips across hers in a tender gesture. "We're getting there."

Her heart thudded when his eyes continued to search hers. What was he seeking within their depths? Indecision furrowed his brow. He took a deep breath, pulled her against him once more and stroked her hair.

"I love you, Kyleigh. I know this may seem too soon since we've only known each other a few months. We've both suffered pain, heartache, and loss. Maybe not in the same way or degree, but nonetheless. We're not children anymore and we both know how short life really is. Too short to not grab hold of a chance for happiness when it's gifted to us."

If her own jealousy stunned her, his declaration sent shock waves through her entire being. "I...ah...."

Lance stopped her stuttering with his finger on her lips. "Don't say anything unless you're absolutely sure. I've said those words to only one other woman in my life and then more out of necessity than true emotion. Hell, I see now that back then I had no idea what love was or could be. What I had with Seth's mother was child's play compared to how I feel about you."

He held her tight a moment then stepped back. "It's too cold to have this conversation here and it's getting late. We'll talk tomorrow."

Kyleigh watched him leave. Though his words had been brave, she couldn't stop the erratic beat of her heart at the dejected slump to his shoulders as he walked away. *Oh, God...God! Dennis! Help me! What do I do?"*

She took a breath, quelled the crazy whirl of her thoughts, and obeyed the command of her heart: Go after him.

"Lance!"

He stopped, turned, and lifted her off the ground as she flew into his embrace. "I love you, too. It's all so new to me. So unexpected. So...I'll ask for us to move slowly, and for time...to know the depths of my own heart before you ask me to give it to you fully."

"Take all the time you need, sweetheart," he muttered between kisses. "I'm not going anywhere."

* * * * *

Kyleigh sat at her table and jotted down ideas for the upcoming year. Lance had driven Ellen and her children to the airport to catch their flight home. The sadness in the woman's eyes, one she understood all too well, had lessened over the days they were here. Even the relationship between Lance and Seth improved daily and the two were often seen laughing and talking while they worked. That, and the changes in Elaina in just a few short weeks, had primed Kyleigh's inquisitive spirit.

Dennis always said there was a therapeutic energy on this ranch. Now she understood. This knowledge fueled her purpose for what they initially thought to be a dude ranch. The Silver Star would be a place of healing and reconnecting with God.

Her stomach growled—and no wonder! She hadn't eaten since last night. Her muscles protested when she stood. Dizziness assailed her. She'd hardly regained her equilibrium when Lance knocked then walked through her doorway. He was beside her in seconds.

"Kyleigh! What's wrong?" Before she could wave him off, he'd pulled out her chair and tried to urge her into it.

"No. Lance, wait. I've been sitting too long and need to move around a little and get the circulation going. That's all."

Her stomach grumbled again. She laughed. "And eat."

Lance glanced down at the paperwork strewn about and picked up a tablet that burst with color as she'd crossed out, highlighted, and switched pens to narrow her focus.

"What's all this?"

"Just some ideas for improving the ranch."

He skimmed through the pages and whistled. "Your talent and imagination are simply amazing."

She'd sketched detailed portrayals of a labyrinth, a small, open-air chapel, and a massage parlor. Her vision for each room—it's setting and décor—were illustrated to the tiniest detail. Some would double as places for meditation or yoga.

"Looks like you've been at this for a while."

"Yeah, I've spent the better part of the day researching, documenting, taking notes, and making phone calls."

He picked up another stack of papers. She'd printed information on equine therapy and other healing modalities that, when coupled with the Word of God, would minister to a person's soul as well as deal with afflictions of the mind and body.

"Equine Therapy? Aren't we doing that already?"

She reached for the information. "I guess in a way we are. But this is more focused. Would you be interested in learning about the process and maybe facilitating events once we get set up? We could send you for training."

"I might. Sounds interesting. Seems like a pretty big undertaking though."

"I know, and I understand it'll take time and effort to implement. Right now, I'm in the planning stage. I'll work on sample ads and brochures, spreadsheets, and calendars so that when I talk to the kids, our attorney, and financial advisors, I'll have every aspect and concern covered."

"I doubt the kids will balk at your ideas. In fact, I'm betting everyone will be on board. The buildings would be easy enough to erect. When do you want to get started?"

She shrugged. "Not sure yet. I'll put these on the altar in my prayer closet and then we can eat."

"Why set them there? Let's show the kids and iron out the details."

His enthusiasm warmed her heart. She smiled and caressed the five o'clock shadow along his jaw with the back of her hand. "Because I want to pray over them and make sure this is God and not just me. I always do this before starting a project of any sort. Especially one that could be so costly."

"Hmph, never thought of that. OK then, you put them away and I'll whip us up something to eat. I'm hungry too."

Three weeks later Kyleigh sat with her family, staff and financial advisor and went over her plans. The overall consensus was a huge GO! Affirmation came when Tess leaned over and pointed to the massage parlor.

"I guess I never told y'all I'm a licensed massage therapist, did I?"

Kyleigh arched a brow at her. "No. You didn't. How long have you been practicing?"

"I've done occasional work for friends and family and fill in once in a while in the shops in Fredericksburg. Still haven't felt comfortable enough in any of those to apply for a full-time position nor do I have enough of a clientele to open my own place. Besides, the drive from where I live into town with traffic and all..." Her words trailed off with a shudder. "But I'd love to do this here! I even have a portable table that fits just about anywhere. I do most of the twelve types of massage."

"There are twelve types of massage therapy?"

Tess laughed. "Yes, but most of them are variations of the traditional. I prefer to stay away from sports and trigger point since those deal directly with injuries, but I can do them."

"Great. We'll work together on packages and pricing for guests and figure your percentage of the fees. In fact, we can start this aspect of our wellness program right away."

"When do you want to implement these retreats?" Robert asked. "And where?"

"I thought we could start small, using the two-room suite upstairs for courses and massages and even one-on-one sessions with our practitioners. Yoga can be out by the pool or in the patio garden area. Nutrition classes would be held in the kitchen. The lodge room is big enough for art, journaling, and vision board sessions."

"That might work," Robert said. "At least until we get your buildings up. The labyrinth would be easy enough to erect, but what about the equine therapy?"

"I've talked with a man who's well known in Arizona. He said he'd be willing to come out on occasion to facilitate an event and he's recommended people in Austin and San Antonio. I haven't spoken with them yet and I have feelers out in other areas. My goal would be for you and Lance to learn this. There are online courses to start but you'd each have to go to a training facility for certification. However, all that can come in time. As long as we can get someone to travel here, we can schedule events. Mr. Redding, the guy in Arizona, will come out to examine our horses and pick the best ones to start this venture. He can also recommend ranches to buy more should we have the need."

"Looks like you've got it all worked out," Ramona said. "What can I do?"

Kyleigh hugged her daughter. "Holistic nutrition shouldn't be hard for you to incorporate. Again, you can be certified online or enroll at the local college. Personally, I think online would be best with the baby and all."

"So do I," Robert and Mona agreed simultaneously, bringing a round of laughter.

"I've never taught yoga but have practiced it for years. Maybe I could get certified in that somehow," Elaina inserted. "I don't know what all is required, but I want to do something special too."

"I'm sure you'll learn a lot helping out with these events and when you decide what that 'something' is, we'll help you get the education and/or training you need." Kyleigh opened her reservation calendar. "We're booked up for Spring Break but have several weeks of free time before and after until Memorial Day. By summer, I'm sure we'll be bursting at the seams."

"Maybe we can start with a couples retreat for Valentine's Day," Tess suggested. "Couple's massages, wine, roses, and chocolate. I have a friend or two I can ask to work with me, or we can get students from Massage Therapy School to do them. They have to get in a certain number of practice hours in order to finish, and this would be the perfect opportunity to get them done."

"That's a great idea," Kyleigh exclaimed. "Gives us a starting point. I'll put brochures and ads together. You guys get that labyrinth set up. I'll contact the Holistic Chamber of Commerce in San Antonio and see if we can get some practitioners out here to help if it turns into an actual event. If not, we'll offer what we can and see what happens."

* * * * *

Six months later, Kyleigh sat in the rocking chair in her daughter's cabin. Her new vision for the ranch had come together so quickly she still couldn't believe it. The Valentine's weekend was a smashing success followed by their first wellness retreat in April.

Kyleigh had brought in a holistic nutritionist, yoga teacher and an energy medicine practitioner. The information provided during those two events spoke so strongly to Elaina, she enrolled for basic energy medicine courses online and took to them like the proverbial duck to water. The practitioner Kyleigh brought out was Elaina's sponsor and would help her with testing and certification.

Equine Therapy sessions had been added. Lance and Robert were not only naturals, but the depths of healing and restoration that resulted from their efforts proved nothing less than amazing. Lance had grown exponentially in his relationship with God, Seth, and her in the process of learning and facilitating the workshops alongside Robert and the man from Arizona.

Today, however, the entire ranch was on pause. Everyone held their collective breath awaiting the arrival of Robert and Ramona's child. She'd opted for a home birth. Kyleigh had held one hand and pressed a wet cloth to her forehead while Robert coached her breathing during and between contractions until the tiny, squalling baby made its appearance. At the moment, Robert and the midwife were getting Mona cleaned up and settled while Kyleigh held her newborn grandson. Emotions collided in her heart, rendering it a jumbled mixture of elation and despair. Tears streamed from her eyes.

Oh, God, such a beautiful child. Do you see him, Dennis? He's so perfect. I wish you were here. The memory of Dennis assuring her he'd held their little one before Ramona conceived brought peace and understanding in a greater degree that they were and would forever be connected in heart and in spirit.

Robert's voice drew her from her musings. "You can come back in now."

Kyleigh cuddled the infant close and rose from the chair just as Lance peeked in from the porch where he, Elaina, and Seth had been pacing. "Well, what's the verdict?"

She smiled. "A boy and he's beautiful."

Robert laughed. "I'd say she's biased but I have to agree with her. Y'all come on in."

Kyleigh handed the baby to his father and allowed Lance to take her hand as they made their way into the room to gather around Ramona's bed. The new mother lay wide awake and glowing.

"Y'all decide on a name yet?" Lance asked.

For months, the couple had tossed ideas but never settled, opting to wait until the child was born before announcing their choice, thinking he or she would help determine the appropriate one.

Ramona smiled up at her husband. "Dennis Kyle, after his grandparents." Her lips trembled, eyes filled. "I just wish dad and the rest of them were here to celebrate his birth and watch him grow up."

Kyleigh embraced her daughter. "Oh, sweetheart, they're all here. They're with us all the time."

Lance wrapped his arms around Kyleigh's waist, then lifted her hand to his lips. In the ten months since he began working at the Silver Star, he'd discovered how Robert's parents, Kyle and Denyse had died when he was a child, leaving him to be raised in a local boys home. "I'd never presume to take anyone's place in your lives, but I'd be honored to be called his grandfather."

He turned Kyleigh in his embrace, dropped to one knee, and pulled a ring out of his pocket. "Will you marry me and give me that pleasure?"

Seth leaned in. "Yeah, and that would make me his uncle."

"And me, his aunt," Elaina chimed. "Once Seth and I get married that is."

Overwhelmed, all Kyleigh could do was nod.

Lance grinned and slipped the ring on her finger as cheers echoed through the tiny house.

The End

If you enjoyed **Kyleigh's Cowboy** you might also like **Lori's Redemption...** Can a notorious bad girl find redemption & win the cowboy preacher's heart? Get Your Copy by Using the QR Code Below!

Want the full blurb? Read on!

Dear Reader,

If you're a long-time fan, you'll recognize similarities in this book and many others set in the Texas Hill Country, particularly the Crossed Penn Ranch/Utopia from **My Heart Weeps** and Bandera from the **Tempered** series.

If you're new to my work, welcome to my world.

The Bible teaches us that God loves us with an everlasting love, calls us by name and stands at the door of our heart and knocks, waiting patiently for us to allow Him entrance.

How many people like Elaina do we know who are lost and hurting? Searching for something or someone to fill the void in their heart. Are we doing our best to introduce them to the only ONE who can make them whole?

Let us strive to be a light in a darkening world and to share the love of God with everyone we meet.

If you don't know Him already, I pray you reach out to the Lord Jesus and invite him into your life. If you do, I hope you'll seek to develop a deeper, more intimate relationship with Him.

Until next time, take care and God bless.

Pamela S Thibodeaux
"Inspirational with an Edge!" ™

About the Author

Pamela S. Thibodeaux grew up in the town of Iowa, Louisiana. She is the mother of four (two by blood and two by marriage) and a grandmother. A deeply committed Christian, Pamela firmly believes in God and His promises.

"God is very real to me, and I feel people today need and want to hear more of His truths wherever they can glean them. People are hungry for practical (and real) Christian values, not some 'holier-than-thou' dictates which are impossible to believe and difficult to live up to," Pamela says.

"I do my best to encourage readers to develop a personal relationship with God. The deepest desire of my heart is to glorify God and to get His message of faith, trust, and forgiveness to a hurting world."

Email Pamela at: pam@pamelathibodeaux.com
Visit her website: http://www.pamelathibodeaux.com
Or blog: http://pamswildroseblog.blogspot.com

Sign up to receive *Pam's Newsletter* and get a FREE short story.

Also: be sure to follow Pam on Social Media: FaceBook, Twitter @psthib, Instagram, Pinterest, GoodReads, and BookBub.

Other Titles by Pamela S. Thibodeaux

Lori's Redemption

Can a notorious bad girl find redemption & win the cowboy preacher's heart?

Lori Strickland (introduced in *Tempered Fire*) has always been known as her father's "wild child" with no desire to change until she meets ex-bull-rider-turned-preacher, Rafe Judson. Her attempts to change her wanton ways come to naught until she realizes redemption only comes with true repentance. Can she find redemption and win the heart of the cowboy preacher?

My Heart Weeps

When life takes everything, your world stops. Can a retreat heal the broken lives of two wounded souls?

Melena Rhyker's world shattered the day her husband died. Lost without the man of her dreams, she digs deep to find a path out of her sorrow. Discovering an artistic retreat, she vows to find a reason to carry on and focus her life in a new direction. Can she heal her own heart, and find her new beginning?

Garrett Saunders knows pain. He's spent most of his life hiding from his past. Regrets and lies haunt him, but he longs to leave them behind and embrace his true self.

Will Melena's efforts to rebuild her life in the face of such grief encourage him to exorcise his own demons of guilt and shame?

Will two hurting people find peace, wholeness and perhaps love in the heart of Texas?

Get this second chance women's fiction novel today and see how love and faith conquers all.

Keri's Christmas Wish

Controversy and Inconsistencies are thieves of holiday joy for Keri...is there any hope for a happy holiday season?

For as long as she can remember, Keri Jackson has despised the hype and commercialism around Christmas—especially with the controversy over the time of Jesus' birth. Will she get her wish and be free of the angst to truly enjoy Christmas this year?

Jeremy Hinton thinks Keri is a highly intelligent, deeply emotional, and intensely complex woman and he's as fascinated by her aversion to Christmas as he is of the woman herself. A devout Christian at heart, he's studied all of the world's religions and homeopathic healing modalities. But when a rare bacterial infection threatens her life, will all of his faith and training be for naught?

Fans of near death experiences will enjoy this woman's mystical journey into spiritual Truth.

Circles of Fate

When two souls are torn apart by duty, can the hand of God bring them back to a happily ever after?

Late Vietnam War era. Strapped for cash, Todd Jameson flirts with disaster. Caught robbing a liquor store to pay for his dad's funeral and given the choice of jail or signing up for the military, he picks the best of two bad options and joins the army. But just as his fresh start reconnects him with a sense of honor and the friendship of a gracious woman, he's deployed overseas into an unknown destiny.

Sixteen-year-old Shaunna Chatman devotes every breath to caring for her sick mother. Working in a diner to make ends meet, the last thing on her agenda is to fall for a young soldier about to be sent into battle. But when he encourages her not to wait, she reluctantly moves on to wed another who's there to pick up the pieces after she buries her beloved mom.

Thrown into a whirlwind of circumstance, Todd flows in and out of the courageous girl's narrative wondering if their stories will ever fully entwine. And though Shaunna's journey grants her a child even as personal tragedy strikes, her thoughts often turn to the boy who still fills her heart.

Will their paths merge once more to bask in the glory of His love?

Circles of Fate is a deeply woven inspirational women's fiction novel. If you like believable heroes, roads to enlightenment, and tales of inner strength, then you'll adore Pamela S Thibodeaux's romantic saga.

Buy *Circles of Fate* to walk in the light today!

The Visionary

Will the ugly secret haunting the twins keep them from finding true love?

While most visionaries see into the future, Taylor sees the past. but only as it pertains to her work. Hailed by her peers as "a visionary with an instinct for beauty and an eye for the unique" Taylor is undoubtedly a brilliant architect and gifted designer. But she and twin brother Trevor, share more than a successful business. The two share a childhood wrought with lies and deceit and the kind of abuse that's disturbingly prevalent in today's society.

Can the love of God and the awesome healing power of His grace and mercy free the twins from their past and open their hearts to the good plan and the future He has for their lives?

Love's Overcoming Power

Temptation, Abuse, Grief, and Doubt are plagues common to women all over the world. In John, 16 Jesus said.... In the world you will have tribulation but be of good cheer, for I have overcome the world.

In this Women's Fiction collection comprised of three full-length novels and one novella, Pamela S

Thibodeaux shares stories that exemplify the power of God's love to overcome whatever situations life throws at you.

Includes: ***The Visionary, Circles of Fate, My Heart Weeps*** and ***Keri's Christmas Wish.***

The Tempered Series Collection

Start at the beginning and follow these beloved characters throughout the years as love crosses the lines of age and strengthens the bonds of friendship. Contains: ***Tempered Hearts, Tempered Dreams, Tempered Fire, Tempered Joy, Lori's Redemption***

Tempered Hearts (book 1 in Tempered series)

An innocent veterinarian. A jaded cowboy. Will they get burned under a Texas sun or find the heat that leads to happily ever after?

Craig Harris has sworn off relationships. He's been burned and betrayed too many times to count. But when he crosses paths with the hot-tempered veterinarian his grandfather hired for the summer will he let go of hurt and mistrust to find the true love he's always longed for?

Tamera Collins is in no mood to put up with an arrogant jerk cowboy even if he is her boss. Grieving too-recent losses leaves her wary of the strong attraction between her and Craig. Can she overcome heartache and shattered faith and open up to their blossoming love?

Tempered Hearts is the first installment of a 5-part family saga where love crosses the lines of age and strengthens the bonds of friendship, and where faith is passed down through the generations proving the sovereignty of God.

Tempered Dreams (book 2 in Tempered Series)

He took an oath to preserve life. Can he stick to it when the woman he loves is in jeopardy?

Dr. Scott Hensley (introduced in Tempered Hearts) has built a wall around his heart since the death of his wife and parents. Katrina Simmons is recovering from scars inflicted on her as a battered wife. Can dreams be renewed and faith strengthened? Can they find joy and peace in God's love and in love for one another?

Tempered Fire (book 3 in Tempered Series)

The daughter of a wealthy rancher… A nobody from nowhere with nothing…Will their love survive?

Amber Harris is a good girl on the brink of womanhood. Stanley Morrison is a young man at the start of his life. For each other, they have always felt the fireworks that two people in love should feel. But the questions about his past, his pride, and Amber's father might be the end of what could be a strong relationship.

As the two try to protect their budding romance, some unlikely but powerful forces conspire to keep them apart. Will they survive the wishes of everyone around them with their relationship intact?

Tempered Joy (book 4 in Tempered series)

He's an 'all around' cowboy. She thinks rodeo cowboys have rocks for brains and a death wish for a soul.

All around rodeo cowboy and heir to the Rockin' H Ranch, Ace Harris is determined not to fall in love. He's only loved one woman in his life, his mother, and no one can even come close to filling her boots. Lexie Morgan thinks rodeo cowboys have rocks for brains and a death wish for a soul. A broken childhood and the death of her father and best friend leave her doubting and questioning God (despite her years of religious upbringing) and afraid of love. Can two young people who clash from the onset learn to trust in the healing power of God and find love and happiness amidst tragedy and grief?

Tempered Truth (book 5 in the Tempered Series)

Will the truth set them free, or will it destroy a lifelong friendship?

Fate declared them neighbors. Scandal insisted they were brothers. The fact that they looked enough alike to be twins only added fuel to the rumors flying about their parentage.

For fifty-plus years Craig Harris and Scott Hensley have enjoyed a bond nothing can sever.

Not the insinuations that they share the same father.

Not the years of strife and grief and heartache.

Not even death.

Will the truth set them free, or will it destroy the friendship that has lasted a lifetime?

Love is a Rose (devotional)

Can God use a secular song to speak to someone and touch their heart?

Music is the magical entry into the spirit world, the golden gate into the Kingdom of God. But we mustn't be of the mindset that God only uses Christian music to reach out and touch our mind, heart, and spirit. God uses any and **every** means available to speak to His children.

Our job is to be open and receptive.

In this devotional, Pamela S Thibodeaux shares how God opened her spirit to a deeper understanding of the abundance of His grace and mercy through the words of the song, The Rose sung by Country & Western artist Conway Twitty.

Pamela offers Seeds to Ponder and a prayer as she parallels the love of God and the Christian life to each verse of the song.

Praise for Pamela S. Thibodeaux

"Pamela Thibodeaux uses her masterful story writing art to create a powerful story of how God heals a woman's heart —broken by grief— through recovery, love and triumph." ~ CBA Best-Selling Author DiAnn Mills on **My Heart Weeps**.

"Loved this book. Wish everyone could read this. Definitely puts all holidays in perspective. If we remember the reason for the holidays then we must put God first.......always. I will certainly recommend this book. Great stuff keep up the great writing." ~ (Amazon) Review of **Keri's Christmas Wish** by Reba

"Oh, the passion, faith and just LIFE that flows through this book...powerful writing indeed!" ~ Review of **Circles of Fate** by Deena Peterson, Book Reviewer @ A Peek at my Bookshelf and Just One More

"Thibodeaux leads the reader through from the first page to the last without once relinquishing control. She hooks them, holds them, and keeps them enthralled until the last line." ~ Review of **The Visionary** by Delia Latham, author of the "Solomon's Gate" series

*"If you have ever considered Christian fiction bland, then check out the **Tempered Series.** It will be well worth your time."* ~ Amanda Killgore for Huntress Reviews

*"**Lori's Redemption** is fast paced, lots of action, gripping storyline... I loved it. It's gone straight back into my TBR pile."* ~ Clare Revell author of the "Monday's Child" series

"Through Pamela's blessed ability to find God everywhere, even in secular song lyrics, she has written devotions guaranteed to touch the heart and remind the reader of our True Love, the Rose of Sharon." ~ Endorsement for **Love is a Rose** by Linda Yezak, Author, Editor Triple Edge Critique Service

Once Again, Thank You.....

I pray you've been blessed as I have by your purchase of this book. If you've enjoyed **Kyleigh's Cowboy,** please write a positive review, and post it at online retailers and websites where readers gather and/or your social media platforms (FaceBook, Good Reads, BookBub, Twitter, etc).

Sign up to receive my **Newsletter** and get a FREE short story.

Temperance
Publishing